For my daughters,
Kirsten and Kelly

The Toothpaste Genie

Sandy Frances Duncan

Illustrations by Susan Gardos

SCHOLASTIC CANADA INC.

Canadian Cataloguing in Publication Data

Duncan, Sandy Frances, 1942-

   The toothpaste genie

ISBN 1-55268-579-9

I. Title.

PS8557.U5375T66 1999   jC813'.54   C98-932843-0
PZ7.D84To 1999

5 4 3 2 1   Printed and bound in Canada   9/9 0 1 2 3/0

Contents

1

What did you expect—
toothpaste?

"Hic!" Amanda's argument was interrupted by a loud hiccup. Her glasses slid down her nose and she pushed them back up.

"Do hold still. I won't be much longer." Mrs. Atkins' voice floated around the large easel.

Amanda giggled. She could see only her mother's legs and it looked as if the easel had its shoes on backwards. In fact, her mother seemed to turn into an easel herself the minute she picked up her paintbrush—a deaf easel with shoes on backwards.

Amanda could feel another hiccup lurking in her throat. She gulped a huge breath and held it while she counted to one hundred, but the hiccup won. It exploded into the room. "HIC!" If she had a glass of water she could drink out of the wrong side ... or if she had a paper bag she could blow into it ... or if she could hold her nose—but she wasn't supposed to move when she was posing. She gave in. "Hic."

"I could get a paper route, Mum. Sandra makes fifteen dollars a month. And I could stop taking piano lessons. How much are they? Eight dollars? Let's see. One a week, that's fifty-two times eight, that's six carry one—uh, forty—uh, four hundred and sixteen. Plus the paper route—twelve times fifteen. What's that Mum? Mum? Mum! What's twelve times fifteen?"

"Mnnm."

Amanda sat straighter. An *mnnm* meant her mother was nearly finished. Good. She tried to wiggle her toes but they were numb.

"What's twelve times fifteen?" she repeated, trying not to move her lips. "Mum?"

"One hundred and eighty."

"So, one hundred and eighty plus—what was it?— four hundred something. Well anyway, that's five hundred and eighty dollars—more like six hundred— and that's every year. We could afford to have a baby then, Mum. We could call her Sarah and she could sleep in my room. I'd look after her. You could capture the *real her* in a picture too. Six hundred dollars more a year so you can have a baby, Mum. Sarah Jane. You'd have Sarah Jane Atkins as well as Amanda Elizabeth Atkins. Okay?"

"No baby." Mrs. Atkins' head appeared around the easel. She had blue paint on her cheek. "You can get down now."

Amanda stood up and stretched. Her leg wrinkled

with pins and needles and she nearly fell. On one foot, she hopped over to the vase and replaced the lilac she'd been holding.

She liked having a mother who was an artist, but she didn't know why it was important that her mother use *her* for a model. The finished picture never looked anything like her. Sometimes she could make out her glasses' frames, other times her long black hair. Once, two years ago, when she'd looked at her finished portrait, she had burst out crying. She hadn't thought she was *that* ugly—all lines and jagged bits. That was when her mother had explained about "capturing the real you" and "the essence of an object." Amanda still hadn't understood, but she had stopped worrying about it.

When she looked at this newest picture all she could see was a giant canvas with smears of blue and purple surrounding hands clutching a bent-over lilac. Mrs. Atkins had accurately caught the "essence" of her bitten nails and scraped knuckles. Amanda wondered if the "real her" was a blue and purple smear.

"No baby," her mother repeated. "We've talked about this before. Even six hundred dollars more a year—and you're not stopping piano lessons, by the way—isn't enough to support a baby. Your dad and I decided on just one baby, and we're very glad she turned out to be the one she did." Amanda returned her mother's smile. "But I've told you babies are expensive and librarians are not exactly well paid—and I am not exactly a financial success as an artist, although maybe I'll begin to sell after the exhibit next month . . . Nope, no baby. Besides, you're ten. A baby wouldn't be much company."

"I didn't mean for *company*." Amanda had heard all this before. She looked at the canvas again. Would a "real" baby be pink or yellow? she wondered. Mrs. Atkins squirted some purple onto her palette and Amanda knew she'd have her attention for only a few more seconds. She decided to give it one last try. "I have to take woodworking in school next year so I could build a crib and a playpen, and I'd save all my clothes so she'd have something to wear. I've always wanted a sister and I'd feed her and teach her things and even if it was a boy that'd be okay—"

"Amanda, *no baby*! And I don't want to talk about it any more. That's it."

Amanda grimaced. She knew from her mother's tone of voice that that *was* it—at least for today. Still, if she got two paper routes, one before school and one after . . . "What did you say?"

"I said, I want you to go to the store. We need bread and milk and cheese." Mrs. Atkins stared at the canvas. "And get some toothpaste you'll use. If I'd been painting a picture of your teeth today, I'd have had to use green!"

Her smile took the sting out of the comment but still Amanda said "Oh, Mother!" and rubbed her tongue over her front teeth. "They're not that bad!"

"Toothpaste," Mrs. Atkins repeated, returning to her canvas.

Amanda took a ten-dollar bill from her mother's purse and added one dollar of her own for a chocolate bar. She wheeled her ten-speed out of the carport and made a flying leap onto the seat. She coasted down the driveway, turned onto the street at a forty-five degree angle, geared down and immediately leaned forty-five degrees the other way to turn off Fourteenth onto Discovery.

It was a glorious day. The sun was shining the way it can only on the first weekend in May, using the half-unfurled chestnut leaves to make patterns on the pavement, heightening the bright reds and pinks of rhododendron bushes, deepening the shadows under cedar trees and beside fences where, it seemed, every preschooler in the neighbourhood was playing. Cats sprawled on warm sidewalks; people pushed lawnmowers or bent over newly spaded soil; teenagers washed cars, radios tuned to the top forty.

Amanda slowed and sniffed the air, sorting out the pungent mixtures of spring: juice of fresh-cut grass, moist and warming dirt, water evaporating on the hot blacktop, car wax, carnations, pansies.

It was a glorious fort-building, ball-playing, kite-flying sort of day, and even if Amanda didn't have a baby sister to put in a buggy and take for a walk or to prop on a blanket on the lawn, the only thing wrong with this Saturday was that she'd spent so much of it inside.

It was a horseback-riding day too, a galloping day, and Flame knew it. He wanted to go as fast as he could, but the blacktop was hard on his hoofs. Amanda stood up on the pedals and tightened the handbrakes to hold him in. He snorted and pulled at the bit, pranced from side to side and gave a playful buck, and Amanda had to guide him around a parked car. They were coming to the hill. She leaned forward over the handlebars, freeing his shoulders for extra speed, and they coasted smoothly with her feet parallel on the pedals as if in stirrups.

Amanda would never have told anyone her bike wasn't a bike: it was a huge chestnut stallion that no one but she could ride. His mother had been killed when he was a foal. Amanda had saved him and raised him, had trained him, and the only one Flame loved was her. He followed her everywhere and she told him everything. Now he cleared the two-metre-high crack in the sidewalk, got only one back hoof wet in the water jump, and galloped down the straightaway to Mr. Fung's store while the crowd cheered on either side. Amanda told him to wait at the bike rack and gave him an extra pat before she went in.

Mr. Fung was busy with a customer, but still he smiled at Amanda. He'd told her once she reminded him of his daughter when she was little, and ever since then he had joked with her when she came in. Not that Amanda thought she was *little*. Still, grown-ups would say "Haven't you grown?" as if they expected her to shrink, and "When I was little..." which was hard for her—even though she'd practised a lot—to imagine.

Amanda sniffed the sweetness of cookies and candies, the richness of coffee, the dusty paperness of kleenex and cereal boxes, and thought that owning a store would be lovely. It always took her a very long time to shop. She had to look at all the products, read the labels, realign tins that had been knocked askew. Sometimes she pretended to play hide and seek in the aisles.

Finally she opened the cooler, took out the milk and cheese, wandered to the bakery shelf for the bread, looked at the kittens on the tins of cat food, and examined the red and greenness of the maraschino cherries. At last she found the toothpaste.

There were four different kinds, all red, white and blue, all priced the same, all with fluoride. Wait. There were five. Hidden behind the red, white and blue cartons and slightly dusty, as if it had lain there a long time, was another box. It was bright purple with green stripes, the only one of its kind. Amanda picked it up, blew the dust off and read the label.

U-Brush-Rite
Guaranteed To Give Pleasure
IMPORTANT: USE ONLY ONCE A DAY

Hmmm, thought Amanda, that's my kind of toothpaste.

"Where did this come from?" Mr. Fung asked when Amanda put her items on the counter. "Have you ever heard of this brand?"

"Nope, but I like any toothpaste you can't use more than once a day. Even once a day is too often!" And, she thought, it looked lonely all by itself on the shelf.

Mr. Fung smiled. He put her purchases in a bag and handed her the change, which she shoved into her jeans pocket. Then she took out her own money to pay for a chocolate bar to eat on her way home.

"I'm here," she shouted as she banged into the house, but the door to her mother's studio was still closed. She put the milk and cheese into the fridge, walked into the hall and threw the toothpaste at the bathroom counter. It missed, bounced off the bathtub and landed on the floor. Amanda grabbed a

8

comic book and went into the back yard to finish her chocolate bar. When she had licked the paper to get every last bit of chocolate, then folded it into very small squares, she remembered what her mother had said and ran her tongue over her teeth. They did indeed feel fuzzy.

Amanda went back into the bathroom for her toothbrush and picked up the toothpaste from the floor. She undid the purple and green carton and put it aside to save. The tube was purple and green too, with *U-Brush-Rite* written in red, old-fashioned writing. The cap was orange. She unscrewed it and squeezed the end of the tube.

A small bubble burped out as if air had been in the tube. The toothpaste was purple too. It seemed to be stuck. She squeezed harder. There was a *pop,* then the bubble started growing and growing and GROWING. Amanda nearly dropped the tube. No skinny snake of toothpaste emerged, just a big purple bubble that grew bigger and bigger, slowly and evenly on all sides. It was now half her size.

Amanda stared at the pale purple bubble. Inside it was a darker purple thing. It was fuzzy at first, but as Amanda watched, its shape became clearer. He (for it seemed to be a he) was fat and had a round head and round, heavy cheeks, a very small nose and short green hair. He sat cross-legged in the middle of his bubble smoking a curved purple pipe.

He was wearing a red loincloth that looked to Amanda like a king-size diaper.

Slowly he took the pipe from his mouth and his face fell into a sulky pout. "A kid! A little kid! I expected someone more important, even if it is my first job!" He took three hard pulls on his pipe. "Well, at least *someone* bought me—even if it is only a kid. Most uncomfortable inside a tube of toothpaste, you know. I don't know why they put me in toothpaste in the first place. Glass jars and lamps are roomier. But you have to change with the times, I guess... If so, why not a coffee pot or a TV or a microwave oven? Can you tell me, hey?"

Amanda just continued to stare.

"It's not polite to stare, little kid. Everyone does it nowadays, but still, it's not polite. What did you expect anyway—toothpaste? Come on, you know you wanted a genie. We don't get bought by just anyone. You have to want us. Oh, will you stop staring and say something!"

Amanda gulped. "Are you a real genie, like Aladdin's lamp genie?"

"Of course I'm a real genie! What do you think— I'm a figment of your imagination? That's what everyone thinks nowadays, but let me tell you," he waggled his pipe stem at her, "no one has that good an imagination. Aladdin's genie was a second cousin four times removed on my mother's side. Poor old fellow—had to work so hard. Aladdin was extremely greedy, never satisfied. And he never once said 'thank you.' I hope you're not like that!"

"Oh no, I'm not like that. At least I don't think so. But I thought Aladdin was nice. He helped his mother and gave things to the poor."

The genie snorted. "That's story-books for you. Distort everything. Sure, he gave his mum some nice clothes and lots of food . . . then he chucked her out on the street so she wouldn't embarrass him in front of the princess. You think that's *nice*?"

Amanda shook her head.

"That stuff about the poor—that was pure fiction. And they always leave the nasty parts out. Do you know what Aladdin did finally?" By now the genie had grown so excited he had worked his bubble into a purple froth. "He broke the lamp my cousin was in! Killed him! Dead! No sir, Aladdin was not nice!"

"I guess they have changed the story then," Amanda said in amazement. "But are you like that? I mean, do you grant wishes and things?"

"Yes, I grant wishes and things. But only once a day. Says so on my label, doesn't it? Union rules."

"You belong to a union?"

"Of course I belong to a union. I might only be an apprentice, but I still work, don't I? I don't want to be taken advantage of. Now, what's your wish? All this talking makes me tired. Genies need a lot of sleep."

Amanda shifted her weight from one foot to the

other. She looked around the bathroom, but her eyes were dragged back to the genie, who continued to stare at her with a bored and irritated expression. The more he stared the less she could think. She bit her fingernail. Finally she said, "I can't think of anything to wish for."

The genie took his pipe from his mouth with a sigh of exasperation and rolled his eyes. "Oh boy, I've ended up with a real winner. What do you mean, you can't think of anything? Everyone can think of something to wish for!"

Amanda realized she was still holding her tooth-brush and placed it on the counter. She *could* think of two things to wish for—a horse and a baby sister —but whoever heard of wishes really coming true? Whoever heard of really wishing with a real genie? How did she even know the genie could grant wishes? And if he could and she wished for, say, a horse, where would she keep it? How would she tell her parents?

No, she couldn't wish for the things she really wanted without giving the problem more thought. That was what she needed, time to think. But what to ask for now that was little, yet would prove the genie really could grant wishes?

If only he would stop staring at her. Desperately she looked around the bathroom for inspiration. Her eyes were drawn back to the purple bubble. If there was a genie in the tube of toothpaste, then there was no toothpaste.

"I wish I had a tube of real toothpaste."

Instantly it appeared on the counter beside the sink.

"You did it! You really did it!" She picked up the tube. It even had a price tag. "Super! Now I wish I had a . . . "

"Ah ah ah." The genie waggled his pipe sternly. "Remember what it says on my label, only once a day and that's it for today. Goodbye." The "goodbye" trailed off as the genie shrank back into his tube. He shrank much more quickly than he had grown. Before he was completely gone he stopped and said in a tiny, shrunken voice, "Don't forget to put my lid on. I'll evaporate."

Amanda carefully screwed on the orange cap. She ran to her bedroom, opened her dresser drawer and shoved the tube under some socks. Then she changed her mind, took it out and stuck it in the very back of her closet under a box of old valentines. No one would ever find it there. Her closet was such a mess.

2

One wish a day

The next morning Amanda woke up thinking about the genie and wondering if today would be a good day to wish for either a horse or a baby sister. She lay curled up in bed watching the sunlight make patterns through the drapes and trying to decide which she wanted more—a horse or a sister—and where she would keep either if she had it. Maybe she should wish for a stable and pasture and saddle and bridle and crib and playpen and diapers before she wished for them. Or maybe, if she said it just right, she could have it all at once in spite of the genie's warning that he would grant only one wish a day.

She flopped onto her other side. The more she thought, the more confused she became. She could hide the toothpaste tube, but how could she hide a baby? Or a horse? She knew the genie had to be a secret—her parents would not like magic. That is, if the genie really was magic. It was all very hard to believe.

The sheet was now hot and sticky and twisted and she felt as though she could not stay in bed one more minute. It was so hard to believe. Maybe yesterday hadn't happened. Whoever heard of genies in toothpaste anyway?

Amanda got out of bed and rummaged in the back of her closet. Pieces of games, jigsaw puzzles, Leggo, Barbie clothes and valentines flew every which way. The tube had not disappeared. She picked it up and turned it over in her hand. An unusual tube of toothpaste—purple and green and red and orange—but still, a toothpaste tube. There was nothing magic-looking about it. Maybe it was full of toothpaste. Maybe the genie had been a figment of her imagination. It wouldn't be the first time that what she'd thought had seemed real. Still, she had to know. She began to unscrew the lid, very aware of its feel between her fingers, aware suddenly of her heart beating fast.

There, it was off. But Amanda's fingers trembled and she dropped it. The lid rolled into the mess on her closet floor and vanished under a comic book. She heard it clunk against some Leggo and bent down to pick it up.

"Would you watch what you're doing, kid! That hurts, you know."

Amanda looked up. The genie was rubbing his elbow. She had apparently banged him against the doorjamb when she bent over. "I'm sorry," she said.

"Yes, well ... " He rubbed it some more so she would get the point. "So, what do you want?"

Amanda's heart was still beating fast and she realized she was scared. There *was* a genie in the toothpaste tube, and that was scary, but the genie was also angry. That made it even scarier.

"What do you want?" he repeated.

"I—just wondered if you were still there—uh, here. Real."

"Course I'm here! Course I'm real! Use your eyes! And you'd better use your eyes and find my lid. Lost it, didn't you?"

"No, I didn't. It's here somewhere." Amanda looked at the floor and nudged the comic with her toe.

"Nope, you've lost it. Just like a kid—can't do anything right. So, tell me what wish you want."

"I didn't want a wish. I just wanted to see if you were here."

The genie glared at her. "You had better learn this *fast,* kid. I'm not a china ornament for you to look at and I'm not a train for you to wonder if it's here yet. I am a *genie* and I grant *wishes*—one a day—and you *cannot* take off my lid and expect me to appear to be admired. I have work to do. I have to give a report at the end of the month and I expect to have some decent wishes to include. So, one wish a day and the rest of the time to sleep. Got that?"

Amanda nodded. She felt about two years old and wondered what she had done to receive such a scolding.

"Now you *have* to wish, so what is it?"

Amanda looked at the floor. The command *to wish* drove all wishes from her. All she wanted was to have him go away so she could sit down. Her knees were shaky. "I wish your lid was back on your tube," she finally said.

And it was. She lay the toothpaste tube in the box of valentines and closed the closet door tightly, then crawled back into bed and pulled the covers over her head. There was no way she could wish for either a horse or a baby if the genie was that grumpy. She would have to think of something else. But already she had used up her wish for the day.

Amanda stuck her head out from under the bedclothes, half expecting to see the genie floating around the room. She paused a moment, then opened the closet door a crack. The tube was lying where she'd placed it. She took a deep breath and slowly her heart stopping banging in her chest. As long as the lid was on, everything was normal. She got dressed.

Mr. Atkins was frying eggs when Amanda came

into the kitchen. "It's a perfect day for fishing," he said. "Don't suppose you'd be interested?" His eyes twinkled."We-ell," Amanda said, playing the game too, "I might be, but I have some important things to do...make my bed, practise my math—you know."

"Things that couldn't be put off. I know." Mr. Atkins flipped over Amanda's egg so it would be hard, the way she liked it. "Don't give it a thought, there'll be lots more sunny days when the salmon are biting. It never rains in Vancouver!"

Both of them laughed at the same time. Amanda threw her arms around her father's waist and squeezed.

Mrs. Atkins was going to stay home and paint, so Amanda and her father made corned beef sandwiches with lots of mustard, loaded the little aluminum boat on top of the car, and drove over Lion's Gate Bridge to Horseshoe Bay.

It was so hot on the water Amanda took off her jeans and sweater, glad she'd thought to put shorts on underneath. While Mr. Atkins got the rods ready, Amanda sat in the stern and steered the boat.

The waves lapped against the bow and made jagged V's behind the stern. The snow-topped mountains reflected the sunlight with a brilliance that hurt her eyes. Amanda felt her rod vibrate as the ocean played with it, like some giant nibbling fish trying to decide whether to take a real bite.

Suddenly her rod dipped and throbbed. She thrust its handle under her knee to give more support. With a great splash behind the boat, a flashing silver salmon leaped out of the water.

"I've got one, Dad! I've got one!"

Mr. Atkins wound in his line so the fish wouldn't get tangled, then reached for the net.

Slowly Amanda reeled in the jerking line. Each time the fish jumped she stopped reeling and held the rod steady with both hands. Then wind again, stop, let the fish play, reel in. Her muscles protested, her hands were sore and blistered. But the fish was tiring too. It no longer jumped so high. It was closer to the boat.

"Come on, fish," Amanda shouted. "I've got you!"

The fish gave one last jump and Mr. Atkins netted it. "That's a real beauty, Amanda. Look!"

But Amanda couldn't look, not while her father clubbed the salmon on the head so it wouldn't suffer. Not while he twisted the hook out of its mouth and gill. Not while it lay there, its valiant, flashing, silver fight all for nothing—just a dead, scaly fish. Amanda's back ached and her hands were still clenched around the rod, but she smiled when her father said, "That was very well done."

Then it was his turn to catch another, just as big.

Later Amanda caught a small one and her father gently put it back.

"We'll get you next year," she whispered as it disappeared over the edge. "Have a nice time till then."

The two salmon in the bottom of the boat already smelled fishy, like hot old spoons. Then Amanda, who loved fishing, who loved looking at fish in the aquarium, remembered she hated eating fish. She even hated touching them, but that was no problem because her father always carried them. But eating them! Too awful for words!

When they arrived home Mr. Atkins took the salmon into the back yard to clean them. Mrs. Atkins, all paint-spattered, came out. "What wonderful fish!" she said. "We'll have one tonight."

At dinner the salmon lay on the platter, headless, tail-less, stuffed and baked, decorated with bits of parsley. Amanda was tired and sunburned and very hungry. As she picked up her fork she thought, Maybe I don't hate fish as much as I used to. I haven't had it in ages.

She did manage to get down one mouthful of the red juicy flesh without gagging, but the next bite seemed to grow in her mouth and the more she chewed the less her swallow worked. Just as her father said, "There is nothing like fresh-caught salmon, especially if you've caught it yourself,"

Amanda coughed, covered her mouth with her hand and hid the mouthful of salmon under the carrots. She filled up on mashed potatoes, and later got ready for bed knowing exactly what to wish for tomorrow.

Before Amanda turned out the light she opened the closet door. The toothpaste tube was lying exactly as she had left it that morning. She closed the door tightly and checked that it was latched, then got into bed and turned out the light. The darkness seemed darker than usual; there was a strange shadow in one corner that she'd never noticed before. She turned on the light and reached over for her teddy bear. He hadn't slept with her for a long time, she thought. He must have been very uncomfortable on the floor.

When her parents came to kiss her goodnight Amanda asked, "Do you believe in magic?"

"What a funny question," Mr. Atkins said. "Whatever made you think of that?"

"I only believe in the magic of art," Mrs. Atkins said.

"What's that?" Amanda asked.

"It's what's true beyond what's real, what's there that we don't see."

Amanda saw her father frown. "You're confusing her, dear. She means is there magic like fairy godmothers and talking fish, don't you?" he said to

Amanda. "Is there magic in the real world? The answer is no."

They kissed her and Amanda snuggled down under the covers. "Please leave the hall light on tonight," she said as her parents left the room.

3

Something fishy

Amanda unscrewed the orange cap. It was the third time she had done it and it felt familiar to her fingers. She wasn't as scared as she had been the day before, but she did hope the genie wouldn't be so grumpy. After all, she thought, he was a genie and his job was to grant her wishes. So she was in charge—she hoped.

"This morning," she said when his bubble had grown to its full size, "I wish I had a never-ending supply of candy."

The genie rocked gently in his purple bubble, smoking his pipe. "I wondered when you'd get around to that! All genies know that if they get owned by kids the first thing they have to do is make like a candy factory. You've been very slow. This will look good in my report." He paused. "But none of this 'never-ending' stuff. All wishes must be concrete and circumscribed." He sounded as if he was quoting a book and Amanda didn't have the slightest idea what he was talking about.

"What do you mean?"

"Look, dummy—"

"I'm not a dummy and I'm not slow either!"

"Sor-ry," the genie said sarcastically. "What I mean is, you can't wish for something to be renewed every day. You can wish for a certain amount and when that's gone wish for more, but a wish won't refill itself automatically."

"But I thought wishes would go on forever."

The genie pursed his lips in exasperation. "Only *some* wishes. Others don't. Not if you need an object refilled. I don't deal in magic pots of porridge!"

"Then I wish I had a very big box of Purdy's chocolates, all soft centres, no coffee-flavoured. Wait, make them all chocolate or maple walnut please."

"Done." The genie's round cheeks grew rounder above his wide smile. "Done, and thank you. This will definitely give me something for my report."

His bubble disappeared. Amanda screwed on the cap, then took it off and shouted "thank you" into the tube. She put it back under the valentines, and when she turned around, there on her bed was the biggest, most purple box of candy she had ever seen. Layers and layers of dark, enormous chocolates. She admired them all before disturbing the arrangement by taking one. It was chocolate-centred. Thick, rich, smooth chocolate. Chocolate again. She ate four more chocolate before she found one with maple walnut. Then she hid the box under her pieces of Leggo and drank three glasses of water in the bathroom.

When Amanda came into the kitchen Mrs. Atkins said, "I've made lots of oatmeal. I know you must be hungry—you didn't eat much dinner." She filled up a bowl and put it on the table.

Amanda slid into her place. She felt a little guilty. Ordinarily oatmeal was her favourite breakfast, but now its familiar smell made her throat close. Her mouth tasted sticky sweet in spite of the three glasses of water. She reached for the jug and dribbled some milk over the heap of porridge. It settled in a circle around it, making the porridge look like an island. Amanda had never considered it before, but porridge was a very strange thing to eat, pasty beige with bits of frothy-looking meal in it. If it had been purple, it would have looked like the genie's bubble when he got angry or excited. Amanda reached for her spoon and excavated a hole in the top of the oatmeal, then made a channel to the edge of the bowl and watched it fill with milk.

Mrs. Atkins saw Amanda's uneaten oatmeal and frowned. Amanda caught the frown and shoved a spoonful of porridge into her mouth. She worked it around with her tongue, then took a drink of milk to wash it down and smiled at her mother. She felt extremely guilty and wished she could offer her mother a chocolate.

"Is that all you can eat?" Mrs. Atkins asked.

"I guess I'm losing my appetite." Amanda choked down one more mouthful and pushed her bowl away.

"Are you feeling all right?"

"I'm fine, but I have to get to school now. Bye."

That night's dinner was a salad made from the remains of the salmon. Amanda picked all the bits of fish out and left them on the side of her plate.

"I don't understand you," her father said. "Salmon is such a delicacy."

Amanda finished the top layer of chocolates before she went to sleep.

The next morning when she came into the kitchen, another whole salmon was lying on the counter.

"I'm going to paint it," Mrs. Atkins said.

"Paint it green and throw it out!" Amanda grumbled, putting some bread in the toaster.

"I'm going to do a still life with the bones from Sunday night's salmon and this whole one. I'll paint it this morning and it'll be thawed for dinner." Mrs. Atkins sounded delighted with herself.

Amanda rolled her eyes and sneered at the salmon. "Its essence will wreck your picture. Dumb fish! I hope you spill paint all over it!"

26

Amanda forgot about the salmon during school, but when she walked into the house after three there it was, back on the kitchen counter staring glassy-eyed at the ceiling, and not a drop of paint on it anywhere. Amanda took the problem to the genie.

"It's just too much," she said when she'd watched the bubble grow. "You've got to make that fish go away. I can't stand to eat it, and I'm going to starve to death! But you can't make it go away fast— that'd look fishy." She giggled. "You have to do it so it isn't too obvious—shrivel it up in the oven or something. Little by little."

"I can't."

"What do you mean, you can't?"

"You didn't say, 'I wish.'"

"*I wish* you'd make the fish go away."

"All right, Amanda, I'll look after it." He puffed gently on his pipe.

She put the toothpaste tube away, had a maple walnut chocolate and went back to the kitchen. The fish's tail was missing. As she watched, more of the fish disappeared. "Little by little" she'd said, she realized with horror. "I meant time, not fish!"

She ran to the bedroom, grabbed the toothpaste tube and tried to unscrew the cap. Her fingers kept fumbling. She tried to use her teeth. The cap would not unscrew.

"Come on out, genie! I didn't mean *that* way!"

The tube started to shake in her hand. Its sides moved in and out very gently and she heard a faint choking sound. Kih-kih-kih. The genie was laughing.

"Oh, you stupid twit!" She threw the tube against the wall. Then she thought, What if Mum goes into the kitchen and sees the fish disappearing! Her first impulse was to crawl under her bed as she had done when she was little, but she ran back to the kitchen.

Now there was only half a fish on the counter. In a minute there was only a head—then only the eyes, which seemed to wink as they disappeared. Amanda felt the counter where the fish had been. She wondered if it had really disappeared or was only invisible.

Just as Amanda was patting the counter Mrs. Atkins walked into the kitchen. Her smile changed to a puzzled frown as she looked around. "That's odd. I left the fish right here." She felt the counter. Amanda drew away and put her hands behind her back. "Very odd," her mother repeated. "I know I put it here."

Amanda smiled nervously. Mrs. Atkins abruptly left the room and Amanda listened to her climb the stairs to her studio. If only he's moved it there, she prayed. She wanted the fish to be anywhere in the house, to reappear on the counter even if she had to go hungry for another night. She wanted that fish now as much as she had not wanted it ten minutes before.

"Okay, Amanda, where's the fish?" Mrs. Atkins came back into the kitchen and checked Amanda's hands, still behind her back.

Amanda shrugged.

"I put it right here." Mrs. Atkins patted the counter. "Didn't you see it?"

"See what, Mum?"

"The fish, Amanda, the fish!"

Amanda didn't know what to say. If she admitted she'd seen the fish disappearing she would have to explain about the genie and she would never be able to have a horse or a baby sister. But if she didn't say she'd seen the fish disappear, her mother would think she was going crazy. Amanda hated the idea of having her mother upset, but she hated even more the idea of losing the genie.

Finally she said, "I didn't see it when it disappeared."

"It really did disappear?"

Amanda wasn't sure whether her mother sounded relieved or more upset. "Maybe it was magic," she offered. "Anyway, it's not there so we can forget about it."

"Forget about it? Either we're crazy or it's the miracle of the millenium and she says forget about it! Fish don't just disappear!" Mrs. Atkins felt the counter again.

Amanda backed towards the door, hoping to escape. "The window's open. Maybe a strange cat got in and ate it. Or maybe Shah ate it! He might have. He *is* a cat."

Mrs. Atkins looked at her daughter for a very long while, as if every gear, wheel and cog in her thinking apparatus was turning over at the same time. "Amanda," she said gently, in a tone Amanda knew well, "what happened to the fish?"

"Maybe you painted its essence too much?"

"Amanda?"

"Mum, honest, I never touched the fish! I hate fish, but I didn't touch it! And I haven't a clue where it is!"

Her mother sighed. "I am very disappointed in you, Amanda. You have always been truthful." Without another word she left the room.

Everything I told her was true, Amanda thought, sniffing back tears. I didn't lie.

But somehow, telling the truth like that felt no different from lying. Having a genie who granted a wish every day was making life more complicated. Amanda would have thought that it would make life easier.

He does things wrong, she thought. Maybe he likes getting me in trouble. But I'll get back at him. Somehow.

4

Parlez-vous français?

It had rained all day, a gentle drizzle that pretended it was not really rain but a damp wool blanket spread out on the treetops, clinging to the children's jackets at recess and coating their faces at lunch. The rain kept up its pretense until three o'clock, when it changed into a tropical downpour that hung straight down in a solid soaking sheet and lasted exactly long enough for Amanda to bike home. She was soaked.

She stripped off her jeans and jacket and socks and left them in a wet heap on her bedroom floor, then sat on her bed in her underwear, eating a chocolate and stroking Shah's thick grey Persian fur while the cat slowly curled and uncurled his paw, making contented rumblings in his throat.

Amanda licked the last of the chocolate off her finger and reached into the box for another. "I wonder what you think about," she said to the cat. "Where do you go at night? Do you have friends? Do you like living with us?" Shah curled himself into a tight ball, then twisted over onto his back. Amanda laughed and scratched his tummy. "I wish I knew what it was like to be a cat."

She jumped up so suddenly Shah opened both eyes and began washing his side in disapproval. Amanda dug around in the back of the closet and snatched out the tube of toothpaste.

"Genie, I wish Shah could talk."

The genie barely had time to open his eyes before he closed them again. "Rhmph," he mumbled as he slid back into the tube.

Amanda replaced the tube, then turned to the cat who was now sitting up on the bed, his tail daintily curled over his front paws. Amanda waited. Shah yawned gigantically, gave one or two cursory licks to his white bib and said, "Qu'est-ce que tu veux savoir?"

"What?"

"J'ai dit, qu'est que tu veux savoir?"

"Oh, that's French. I can't understand it. Speak English."

"Pardonnez-moi?"

Amanda, who had had two periods of French every week since September, said, "Um—parlez-vous —um—anglais?"

"Non, je parle français," Shah replied in an irritated tone, lying down and preparing himself for another nap.

"Oh, snort." Amanda pulled out the toothpaste tube again.

"What is it now?" the genie asked.

"You made him speak French, for goodness sake, and I can't understand him!"

"All right, all right, there you go! Now leave me alone—for goodness sake yourself!"

Dumb genie, Amanda thought as she screwed the cap on for the second time. I wonder if Aladdin's genie was grumpy too. "Shah, can you understand me now?"

"Of course. I actually speak three languages: Cat, French and Arabic, plus Persian Cat, a dialect combining Cat and Arabic."

"What's it like being a cat?"

"Quite nice. What's it like being human?"

Amanda shrugged. "Okay, I guess. I don't think about it much."

"There you are. Neither do I. One just is what one is." Shah turned around and lay down on his other side.

"Please don't go to sleep. Tell me about being a cat."

Shah sighed. "Being a cat is being fast, well coordinated, patient, independent and clean, sleeping when necessary, catching mice and birds, and *not worrying about what it's like being a cat*!"

"What do you do when you go out?"

The tip of Shah's tail flipped back and forth. "I go for a stroll, check out the neighbourhood, see what the other cats are up to, perhaps catch a mouse—the usual sorts of things."

Shah was not a very interesting conversationalist, Amanda thought, but she persisted. "What do you think about?"

"When?"

"Any time. When you're chasing a mouse. Now."

"When I'm chasing a mouse I'm thinking about chasing the mouse, or perhaps catching the mouse. Now I'm thinking I wish you'd stop asking questions." Shah noticed Amanda's look of disappointment and added in a kinder tone, "Look, I like living here. You're a quiet family and feed me well and don't disturb me—much. And I mind my own business as I think everyone—cat or human—ought to do. We cats don't analyze things much. Why don't you be a good girl and go find something to do?"

Amanda could see she wasn't going to get any farther with Shah. If that was all a cat had to say for itself it wasn't very interesting, and the waste of a good wish. She pulled on some dry clothes, took another chocolate and went into the living room.

It was talk-show time on television. Amanda kept flipping the dial. There was only one program that looked interesting this time of day, a cartoon show with cows and dancing chickens, but Amanda flipped by it—it was on the French channel. She turned the dial around again, this time more slowly, and again passed the dancing chickens. Suddenly she stopped and twisted the dial back. She could understand what they were saying. Amanda backed into a chair and curled up. It was quite a funny show now she knew what it was about.

Mrs. Atkins came down the stairs from her studio. "Hello, dear," she said to the back of Amanda's head. Amanda half turned in her chair and waved her arm at her mother. Mrs. Atkins went into the bathroom and Amanda could hear the shower.

By the time her mother came out, the cartoon show had changed to an old man in a rocking chair telling a story about when he was young. Amanda switched off the set.

Just then the front door opened and Mr. Atkins walked in.

"Bonjour, Papa." Amanda threw her arms around him.

Her father looked puzzled, then laughed and hugged her back. "Bonjour, chérie. How was your day?"

"Très bien, merci. Comment ça va?"

"Very impressive French, Amanda," Mrs. Atkins said. "Hello," she said to her husband, kissing him.

"You've been practising, eh?" Mr. Atkins said.

"Non, Papa, pas beaucoup." She frowned. She wasn't speaking French—she thought. Now she tried again. "Aujourd'hui j'ai eu la meilleure note de la classe en mathématiques." Although that was exactly what she had wanted to say in English while it was in her head, she could tell by her parents' puzzled expressions that it had come out in French.

Mrs. Atkins, who said she could read French, repeated, "Aujourd'hui . . . oh." She turned to Mr. Atkins. "She got the highest mark in math today."

"I bet you did in French too," her father said.

Amanda was beginning to worry. She tried very hard to speak English, thinking it through first in her head. After all, she could understand them and they were speaking English, and her thoughts were going around in the usual way. It was just coming out differently. "Qu'est-ce qu'on va avoir pour le dîner?"

Her parents smiled at her as if she was four years old and had said she had a yellow invisible rabbit named Harold and they were supposed to pretend to see it too.

Mrs. Atkins said, "Pour le dîner nous—um—aurez du bifteck, des pommes de terre rôties, et—um—des petits pois."

Amanda turned away so her mother wouldn't see her smile. Mrs. Atkins' accent was dreadful and she'd made a grammatical mistake. Not that

Amanda would tell her so for the world; she didn't want to hurt her feelings and her mother sounded so pleased with her attempt. Her parents thought it was a game. But it wasn't a game—she could no longer speak English.

She felt furious with the genie. All sorts of words she didn't think she knew—in French or English— were in her head. This was the second simple, reasonable request he had messed up. Did she have to spell everything out for him? Didn't he know how to make a fish disappear? Didn't he know enough to make a cat talk English instead of having her talk French? What sort of a genie was he? Amanda could see nothing funny in it. Except her parents' accents.

Now Mr. Atkins was trying. "Ma petite fille—"

Amanda broke into a laugh. Fortunately, so did her mother. Then her father.

"That wasn't so bad, was it?" He tried to sound hurt, but his eyes were twinkling.

"Oh, Papa, c'était très mauvais."

"What did you say?"

"J'ai dit—"

"You should say 'pardon' or at least 'quoi,' dear," Mrs. Atkins interrupted.

"Oh fiddle!" Mr. Atkins went into the kitchen and poured a glass of juice.

"Really, Amanda," Mrs. Atkins said, "I can't get

over your French! You sound as if you've had an immersion course. Mr. Bates must be an excellent teacher."

Amanda giggled at the thought of Mr. Bates, with his bald head and thin lips, saying the words that had been in her head a few minutes before. She hadn't known exactly what they meant, but she had known that they were definitely not nice.

Mr. Atkins came back with some crackers and peanut butter. Amanda took one. "We'll have to go to France," he said. "You can translate for us."

Just then Shah padded down the hall and into the living room. He looked at Amanda and said, "You are just about to get into trouble."

"Feed that cat, Amanda. He sounds hungry," Mrs. Atkins said, and Amanda realized her parents thought Shah was only meowing.

"Pourquoi?" Amanda asked Shah.

"Don't ask why. You know. And I'm not hungry, although now that you mention it, a little nibble of something tasty might suit. Is there any of that delicious tuna left?" He started toward the kitchen hopefully.

"Amanda, feed the cat—and do stop speaking French. I'm tired of it." Mr. Atkins was now juggling the newspaper as well as the plate of crackers.

"*That's* what I mean." Shah jerked his head towards her father and then licked his shoulder.

"I don't know why that dumb genie made me

speak French," Amanda complained while she found a tin of tuna.

"Better than Arabic, isn't it?" Shah said. "After all, you wanted to talk to me. Suppose it was Cat. What would your parents think if you could only meow?"

"Well, he'd better change me back—and fast!"

Mrs. Atkins came into the kitchen in time to hear the last, which sounded to her like "et vite."

"Oh, good grief," Mrs. Atkins said. "You *can* still speak English, can't you?"

"Certainement, Maman!"

Shah at that point had a sneezing fit. Amanda glared at the cat, tried to smile at her mother, and sidled out of the kitchen.

"Come back here and set the table, Amanda. Dinner's nearly ready."

"Un moment, un moment. J'ai quelque chose d'important à faire!"

Amanda slammed her bedroom door, dug out the toothpaste tube and savagely ripped off the lid. "You make me speak English right this minute, do you hear?"

"Pardon? What did you say? I don't speak French, you know." The genie's face was a deep mottled purple, and he rocked back and forth in his bubble holding his sides. "Your parents are so proud of you! You should teach them French too!"

"Oh, shut up! You and your stupid dumb jokes!

Just you wait! Now you make me speak English or else!"

"Threats, Amanda? That's not nice. Besides, you've used up your wish for today. Technically, you've had two."

"Well, I'm going to have a third or I'm taking you into the living room like this!" She waved the tube around and the genie rattled from one side of the bubble to the other. The tobacco dropped out of his pipe.

"Watch out!" He fished around the bottom of his bubble for the hot coal, moving faster than Amanda had ever seen him move. Finally he scooped it up in his pipe and said, "You nearly burned me!"

"Ve-ry sor-ry! Now—English. Or do we go into the living room where my mother will see you and take you away to her studio and make you stay up all night so she can put you in a picture? To say nothing of what my father might do!"

They glared at each other for a minute, then the genie looked away. "Oh, all right. But you won't be able to talk to the cat."

"Who cares? He didn't have anything interesting to say anyway."

"I could have told you that in the first place."

"Why didn't you?"

"You didn't ask."

Amanda had a sudden inspiration. "How about making me able to talk French and English?"

"Oh no, no, no!" And *zip,* the genie and his bubble were back in the tube.

Amanda smiled. "I didn't think you would, somehow."

5

A neat wish

Amanda had had the genie for over a week and had not yet wished for a horse or a baby sister. At first she'd used her wishes to see if the genie really did grant them, but after the fish disappeared and after her talk with Shah, she realized she didn't trust the genie. He *had* given her what she wished for, but the way he did it was sneaky. Just as if, she thought, he really enjoyed the idea of getting her into trouble.

Amanda's best thinking time was first thing in the morning before she put her glasses on, almost as if she could see things inside her head more clearly if everything outside was still fuzzy. Suddenly she thought of something she hadn't thought of before. There *was* a way she could have everything at once.

Amanda jumped out of bed, but then it struck her that it was Monday morning. She crawled back under the covers. She did not want to go to school.

It wasn't that she didn't like school. She had always liked it—more or less. Right now it was less.

She seemed to do nothing but get into trouble with Mrs. Hayward. Not because she couldn't do the work; she'd always been good at schoolwork, especially reading and math, and very good at talking. Mrs. Hayward said she was the best talker in the class.

But Amanda was terrible at writing. Not like Cynthia. Cynthia had the most beautiful handwriting. She could write anywhere—with or without lines, even on the board—and it looked neat. Cynthia could draw people too, and the funniest looking monkeys. But not Amanda. It seemed that every time Amanda picked up a pencil or pen or crayon it grew a mind of its own, and its mind was full of blotches. Amanda's work was always messy, even when she tried her hardest to be neat. *Especially* when she tried her hardest. It was very discouraging. And with a mother who was an artist, as Mrs. Hayward kept saying, you'd think Amanda would be neater.

On Friday, she had very nearly cried in front of the whole class when Mrs. Hayward held up her science report on whales and said she wouldn't accept anything so messy and for Amanda to do it over. And what had been even worse, if anything could be, was the I'm-so-smart-and-you're-so-dumb expression on Cynthia's face.

That was why Amanda still sat half in and half out of bed on Monday morning. Right after math she had to face redoing her report. Already the first paragraph, which she'd started Friday afternooon, had three blotches, and a hole where she'd erased. If only she could write neatly.

"That's what I'll wish for," she said, completely forgetting her previous idea. Amanda put on her glasses so she wouldn't trip over the mess on her floor, and took out the toothpaste tube. She undid the cap. Slowly, ever so slowly, the purple bubble began to grow. Amanda bristled with impatience. She could just about see the genie inside the bubble. His eyes were tightly closed. He rubbed them, blinked a few times and yawned.

"It's about time! You took so long I thought I was hibernating! You're supposed to use me every day. Anyone but a little kid would! On the other hand, what do you mean, waking me up so early? I need my sleep, you know!"

Amanda felt so confused she started to apologize, then stopped, since she didn't know what to apologize for.

"Can you make me as neat a writer and drawer as Cynthia?" she asked, and with sudden inspiration added, "Make me all neat. Make my shirts stay tucked in, my socks not wrinkly and my hair stay combed—and easy to comb too. And how about my bedroom?" She looked at the litter: toys, a half-eaten cookie, clothes on the floor mixed with her bedspread, her bed full of lumps. "Can you make it neat too?"

"No! That's too many wishes. I told you only one. Union rules."

Suddenly Amanda heard footsteps coming down the hall. She threw the genie into the closet, closed the door and leaned against it.

Her mother opened the bedroom door. "Aren't you dressed yet? It's after eight. And who were you shouting at?"

"No one." Amanda crossed her fingers behind her back. "No person." The genie wasn't really a person, she reasoned. "I was—uh—practising."

Mrs. Atkins didn't look convinced. "Just hurry up now, and by the way, I want this room cleaned up today. It's worse than a pigsty."

"Yes, Mum. I'm working on it now." She leaned hard against the jiggling closet door.

Mrs. Atkins opened the bedroom door more widely. "Don't start it now, Amanda, or you'll be late. Do it after school . . . And why are you rattling the door like that?" She took another step into the room and there was a dreadful noise from the closet as if everything in it had started to dance around.

The pressure on the door was more than Amanda could bear. Just as her mother started across the room Amanda yelled, "The stove! I can hear the timer!"

"Drat, that'll be the eggs. Now get dressed or yours will be cold."

As her mother closed the bedroom door Amanda opened the one to the closet. The purple bubble had grown to an immense size and was frothing. All the toys, books and games which had teetered precariously on Amanda's shelves were now on the floor. The toothpaste tube had a dent in the bottom.

"Thank you very much," the genie said icily. "How would you like to be unceremoniously chucked into a messy closet like that when you're only trying to do your job?"

"I'm very sorry, but I didn't want my mother to find you."

"She might know how to treat a genie better than you do."

"Oh no, she wouldn't. She'd want to paint you. You'd have to pose. She'd capture your essence."

"My what?"

"Your essence. The real you."

"The real me?"

"That's what she does. She's an artist."

The genie rolled his eyes. "She sounds more dangerous than you!"

"She's not dangerous, she's really nice. But she makes you pose and that's boring. You'd have to sit still . . . and she wouldn't let you go to sleep."

"Not sleep! Well!"

"Now, about my wish," Amanda said, feeling more in control. It was apparent one had to be firm with genies.

"All right, your wish, but be quick." He looked toward the bedroom door as if expecting Mrs. Atkins again.

Amanda's brain had shifted into high gear. "I wish you would make everything about me, including what I do, neat. That's only one wish, isn't it?" She smiled persuasively.

The genie held his pipe in his hand and rubbed his nose. "You are a tricky one." He frowned. "It's highly irregular, but I guess it's all right. Just don't try it too often. At the end of the month I have to give a very important report, you know." He disappeared into his tube with amazing speed and Amanda replaced the orange cap.

Suddenly everything in her room began to fly around, bumping and jostling for position. The pieces of games sorted themselves out from the jigsaw puzzles and crashed into the right boxes. The boxes flew onto the shelves. Amanda watched the bed make itself, the dolls walk over to the wall and line up, the dirty clothes fly into the laundry hamper and the clean ones into the drawers. In the midst of this her nightgown undid itself and flew under the pillow and her school clothes took its place. It was like the cyclone which had carried

Dorothy to Oz. Amanda hung on to the closet doorknob for fear of being tidied away as well.

Slowly the room quieted. Amanda had never seen it so neat. She had never known it had so much floor space. She had only to empty the wastepaper basket.

"That was fast," Mrs. Atkins said approvingly when Amanda appeared for breakfast. "And don't you look nice. How did you do your hair?"

"I don't know," Amanda replied truthfully. As she sat down at the table she automatically reached up to readjust her glasses, which usually slipped when she bent over. But this time her glasses did not slip. Her hair did not flop onto her plate. Her knife did not fall onto the floor. She was able to put jam on her toast without slopping it on the table and she was able to get the lid back on the jam pot without getting the outside sticky.

Amanda felt neat. She felt so neat she wondered if she had been pasted together. Her socks were snug around her knees and from the tightness of her shoes she knew the laces were still done up. She wondered if she wasn't a bit too neat.

It was windy outside, but neither that nor her fast bike ride to school dislodged one hair on her head.

The real test of the wish came when Amanda picked up her pencil for math. She actually had a pencil—and a pen and an eraser, she discovered, checking her desk. Not only did she have them; they were all in her pencil case. Her books were neatly organized—texts on one side, exercise books on the other—stacked so she could pull one out without having the rest fall onto the floor. Right on top was last week's spelling list which she'd told Mrs. Hayward she'd lost.

Amanda opened her math book, turned to a clean page, took a deep breath and quickly wrote her name and the date on the top line.

Amanda Elizabeth Atkins   Monday, May 11

It was beautiful. The letters all slanted the same way and were all the same height. Somehow she had produced a small elegant curlicue on each capital. It looked as beautiful as Cynthia's writing. No, *more* beautiful. The genie was really and truly magic. It *would* be possible to have a horse and a baby sister. It was all in how she said the wish.

Humming quietly to herself, Amanda finished the page of multiplication, then took it up to the teacher's desk, noticing that Cynthia was still working. Amanda took out her library book. As she read, her hand automatically began to fiddle with a strand of hair. But the strand wouldn't be fiddled with. As soon as she separated it from the rest of her hair and wound it around her finger, it unwound and snapped back into place. She took three strands and tried to braid them. But again, as soon as she had two strands braided, the third slipped back and while she was fiddling with it the other two unwound and again assumed their neat, well-combed place down her back.

Oh well, she thought, it sure won't get messy.

She settled herself in front of her book again and absentmindedly started biting a fingernail. But she had read no more than a paragraph when she realized something felt strange against her tongue and teeth. She took her finger out of her mouth and looked at it. The nail had grown back.

Amanda carefully bit it down to the quick. It grew back. She nibbled again. Somehow it seemed harder to bite, as if it was growing thicker. She looked at it again. This time the nail had grown both faster and longer. She frowned and with determination bit it again, but the more she bit it, the longer it grew. Soon it protruded a ruler's width over the end of her finger, then two, then three.

Amanda glanced around the classroom, then quickly shoved her hand under her leg, scratching herself with the giant nail as she did. Her heart beat faster and her cheeks felt warm. How was she going to get the huge fingernail into her mouth to give it a really good bite without anyone noticing? If she couldn't bite the nail off she'd have to keep her hand hidden all day, but her hand was feeling ginger ale fizzy from the pressure of her leg. No one was looking at her. She withdrew her hand and shoved it in her desk. The enormous fingernail clanked against something. Her scissors! She reached for them with her other hand and in the dark of her desk, by feel alone, cut the nail to a comfortable length. She drew her left hand out and watched anxiously. Nothing happened. The nail didn't grow.

Amanda slumped down in her chair and let her breath sigh out. It was the most peculiar cure for nail-biting she had ever heard of. In turn she nibbled each of her other nails until they too had grown to a comfortable length. She spread her hands on the desk top and admired their new look.

"Amanda," Mrs. Hayward called from her desk, holding the page of multiplication. "This has your name on it, but it doesn't look like your work. It looks more like Cynthia's. How did you do it?"

"I don't know," Amanda said for the second time that morning. And it was true. She didn't *really* know. "I guess I'm getting neater." She smiled.

Mrs. Hayward did not smile back. Instead, she frowned. Seriously. Suspiciously. Questioningly.

Amanda bit her lip. "It *is* my book."

"I know it's your book," Mrs. Hayward flipped back to the previous week's math, "and this is your work"—she turned to today's—"but this doesn't look like your work."

"Well, it is." Amanda's hand crept to her mouth and she bit her nail. Immediately she could feel it growing.

The teacher handed Amanda a pencil. "Show me how you did it."

Amanda recopied the last question, then wrote her name at the bottom of the page. The curlicues on the capitals had an even greater flourish.

"It's fantastic!" Mrs. Hayward said. "How did you do it? You must have practised all weekend!"

"Oh, no, but I did want to be neater."

"Well, it's lovely, I'm sure."

Amanda looked at her teacher. The tone in which she had said that sounded as if she didn't think it was lovely at all.

After recess Mrs. Grower, the principal, came into the room. She wandered around pretending to look at all the children's work, but Amanda knew Mrs. Grower was there because she had become neat. Eventually the principal arrived at her desk, smiled, and looked at the report on whales that Amanda was copying. Then she picked up the old report and compared them. "You've certainly improved, Amanda."

Amanda heard her whisper to Mrs. Hayward, "It's probably nothing to be concerned about, but you could phone her mother."

Amanda had just walked into the house for lunch when the phone rang. She heard her mother say, "Too neat?...That suddenly?...Yes, it is hard to believe...But people change. She's probably been working on it and we didn't notice...Too sudden? ...Well, she's always been neat inside, if you know what I mean...You don't know what I mean? Well, the *real her*...Yes, we'll keep in touch, but don't worry. Sometimes people change fast...Yes, it is wonderful..."

Amanda slipped out the door and banged it coming in so her mother wouldn't know she'd overheard.

"Hello, dear," Mrs. Atkins said. "Thank you for cleaning your room. You did it so quickly!" Then she put her arms around Amanda and said in a choked tone, "Don't grow up too fast. We love you just the way you are. You don't have to change."

Amanda sighed. Here everyone had been telling her for years she was so messy and careless, and now when she finally became neat, they thought she'd changed too much. Grown-ups! She couldn't figure them out.

6
It's not allowed!

"Genie," Amanda said the next morning when she'd watched the purple bubble grow, "I wish I could have ten wishes a day." That had been her good idea of the day before, the one she'd forgotten to wish when she decided she wanted to become neat.

The genie pinched his lips together and frowned so ferociously his green eyebrows formed a single unbroken line like a border of grass. He shook his head. "No. One wish a day. It's in the rules."

"It is only one wish," Amanda said. "It's my one wish for today."

"No. You can't make that sort of wish."

Amanda had thought he might be difficult. She made herself as tall as possible, gripped the toothpaste tube firmly and looked the genie straight in the eye. "Now, look. *You* are a genie and *I* am a person and you have to do as I say. I'm the boss."

The genie clamped his pipe stem between his

teeth, sighed and looked away. "I knew this would happen with a kid," he mumbled. "Inconsiderate, thoughtless little ... " Amanda could hardly hear him.

"What's wrong with my wish? It's only one. I'm following the rules. And I *am* the boss." She liked the sound of that very much. "It'd look good in your report," she added.

"What's wrong with it! Do you want to know what's wrong with it?" The bubble had expanded and was beginning to froth. Amanda held the tube at arm's length. "I'll tell you what's wrong with it! You'll wear me out, that's what's wrong! Where do you think wishes come from, anyway? You think wishes are sitting out there in English Bay and all I have to do is snap my fingers and they roll up like waves? Is that what you think? Well, it isn't like that! Magic is hard work! That's why I get tired. That's why genies have a union!"

"I didn't know," Amanda said. "And you don't have to get mad!"

They stared at each other and slowly the bubble got smoother. "Ten wishes a day," the genie said more quietly. "Each day. That means I have to work ten times as hard, because I have to fill each of those wishes—technically, it'd mean eleven wishes a day. I'd be worn out; there'd be nothing left of me to graduate. That's why the union banned it. That's why all wishes must be concrete and circumscribed —it's covered under that rule, by the way. You stretched it pretty far yesterday with your neat wish. That was *not* easy, especially in your case. Some wishes are tougher to grant than others."

"What if I wished for ten easy-to-grant wishes a day?"

"No. Absolutely not. The union wouldn't like it, and the Master Genie wouldn't like it. I can just see my report." The genie rubbed his hair and said in a mocking tone, "I had this little kid, see, and I let her talk me into ten wishes a day—Why, I'd be laughed at! One wish a day, and that's enough trouble. Now, what's it going to be?"

"I didn't know all that," Amanda said. "I've never had a genie before. I don't know anything about magic. Is it all hard work?"

"Very hard work. So is talking and talking. What do you want?"

"There are two things I want—"

"So, one today and one tomorrow." The genie closed his eyes.

"—but I keep having to use wishes for other things. Like now. I have to do a report so I have to wish it was done." Amanda sighed. Mrs. Hayward had said all reports were due for certain tomorrow. Hers was to be on Indian legends. So far she had only one paragraph written. Of course, Cynthia had handed her report in last week. The only way

56

Amanda could have hers ready was to wish it done. But the genie had dozed off.

"Genie!" Amanda rattled the toothpaste tube and he jerked awake. "I want you to write my report."

"Write *your* report? I'm having enough trouble with my own. Anyway, I can't. It's against the rules. We aren't allowed to do anything for anybody they can reasonably do for themselves."

"Your *rules!* You change them all the time! I thought you probably wouldn't do it. You never do anything useful."

"What do you mean by that? I do so! Besides," he added suddenly, "I can't write."

"Oh, come on. Everybody can write."

"Genies aren't everybody. It's not considered necessary."

"What do you mean necessary? How are you going to do your report?"

"There's more than one way to communicate. Genies use thought transference."

"What do you mean?" Amanda repeated.

"I'm not really allowed to explain, but when we genies are together we can read each others' thoughts. Our meetings are nice and quiet. No yelling. No eye strain from reading fine print."

"Maybe you could transfer the thought to Mrs. Hayward that I did the report and got an 'A'?"

"Wouldn't work. She's not a genie. Anyway, we deal in reality. We can't change what hasn't happened. If you'd done the report I could give it to someone half a world away or a million years ago. I could make it disappear. I could turn it inside out or rewrite it backwards. But if you haven't done the report then it doesn't exist and there's nothing I can do." He started to curl himself up, preparing to shrink into the tube.

"Wait! Please don't go. She'll kill me if I don't do the report!"

The genie sighed. "That's hardly likely. Teachers don't *kill* students. Do try to say what you mean."

"You know what I mean." Amanda could feel tears beginning.

"Look, you can do it. Your mum or dad can help you. Anyway, this is most irregular. I'm here to grant wishes, not act as an advice bureau. One wish a day and the rest of the time to sleep. Union rules."

"Stupid union," Amanda muttered, the tears now trickling down her cheeks.

"Do stop crying. You'll get me all wet! Oh, good grief, you obviously don't know how to use a genie properly, even yet. Nobody does nowadays ... but that's beside the point. I can't write your report for you and I can't make Mrs. Whosit think you've done it if you haven't. Apprentices' powers are limited, you know. If you need to know about something that's happened, all I can do is transfer you where you can see for yourself."

"You mean I could go there? But how do I get there? How do I get home again?"

"That's my department."

"But my parents will miss me. I don't want them to worry."

"Amanda, I am losing my patience, and I am very tired." The bubble began to froth again. The genie puffed on his pipe for a minute. "You know how slowly time goes when you're doing something you hate?"

Amanda nodded.

"And when you're having fun, time goes too quickly?"

She nodded again. "But I don't see what that has to do with my report."

The genie sighed and took his pipe out of his mouth. "Time is like an elastic band. It can be stretched or twisted or folded up. And time can be different for different people. What I mean is, it can be long for you and short for your parents at the same time." He laughed. "They don't even have to know you're gone. So stop worrying and say where you want to go."

"The report is on an Indian legend—"

"And do hurry up! I could have granted a thousand wishes in this time. All this talking exhausts me."

"I have to go to some Indians then."

"If you want to visit some Indians, go call on the Georges in the next block—or the Shankars. They're Indian too."

"I don't mean Indians like now. Besides, the Shankars are from India. I mean Indians like before —longhouses, totem poles, that kind of Indian." Amanda waited. "Well?" she began.

"Jumping Geniacs!" the genie yelled. "Can't you ever remember to say 'I wish'!"

"I wish!" Amanda shouted back.

Her stomach heaved and she swallowed against the nausea. Her legs felt weak and her head dizzy. She closed her eyes and was aware of darkness and a sharp, smoky, sweet-sour smell. After a while she opened her eyes.

She could make out a fire in the middle of an enormous building, around which people danced slowly and rhythmically in some ceremony. They wore long cloaks decorated with jewels or shells which broke and reflected the firelight. On their heads they had masks, grotesque and frightening. One she recognized as a bird because of the long pointed beak; another mask was round and had a human face.

Amanda was sitting in the midst of a group of girls and women, resting against a ledge. Opposite her, across the fire pit, sat more men and women, some of whom beat great round drums. One was shaking a rattle and the rest were chanting.

60

Amanda looked up. A huge, dark shape floated down from the smoke hole in the roof. Very slowly it descended until it was directly over the fire; then it settled and spread until the fire went right out.

The blackness was total. Children screamed. Close by, a woman shrieked. Amanda threw herself under the ledge against which she'd been leaning, closed her eyes and tried to curl up as small as possible. It seemed that the screams and scurryings continued forever, but then, just as gradually as the fire had gone out, it rekindled itself. Soon the centre of the longhouse was as brightly lit as before.

Amanda peeked out. There were fewer people, only men and boys. There were no females of any age—except her. Just as Amanda realized this, so did the men. Some ran for the door; some of the little boys began to cry. The chief looked horrified. As Amanda watched, he was approached by a very old bent man in a shell-covered cloak who took the talking stick and rapped the end on the floor. Amanda decided this must be the shaman, the most revered person in the tribe.

"It was Raven who stole the women! He must be angry and is playing a trick to punish us! We will have a council." The shaman sat cross-legged by the fire and slowly all the men joined him. The boys sat in a circle behind them.

A draft caught the smoke and directed it towards Amanda, making her sneeze. She tried to shrink under the ledge some more, but there was nowhere for her to go.

The young chief peered under the platform, then pulled her out by the leg. "Little Dove! How did Raven not get you?"

Amanda stood up, her face turning red under the stares of the men. Who was this Little Dove? She sneezed again and rubbed her nose. She realized she was missing the familiar weight of her glasses, yet she could see perfectly.

The shaman nodded at her. "She must be in Raven's favour."

"I hid," Amanda whispered, not wanting to give the wrong impression.

But no one listened. All watched the shaman as he sat by the fire, powerful and mysterious, with the light playing over his strong-featured face. Amanda sat down. Her knees felt watery.

"We cannot outfight Raven," the shaman said. "We must outsmart him. Little Dove has been left behind, so her magic must be strong. We will think through the night what we must do. In the meantime, guard the girl well."

Amanda looked around again for Little Dove. Then her interest changed to fear. "I must be Little Dove," she realized with horror. Before she had a chance to tell the council she was really Amanda Elizabeth Atkins, two men took her by the arms and carried her to the farthest corner of the sleeping platform, where they spread a bearskin rug and said, "Sleep."

I want to go home, she thought desperately. I have enough information for my report. Genie, I want to go home!

Faintly, as if from far away, she heard the genie snicker. "You can't go home in the middle of a legend! Union rules!"

I bet the genie makes up the rules, she fumed. There always seem to be new ones. Now I guess I have to stay. Amanda pulled some of the bearskin over her. It was soft and warm and she soon grew used to the strange, smoky smell.

She just hoped she could finish the legend without becoming a permanent part of it.

7
Alias Little Dove

"Little Dove, wake up." The Chief shook Amanda gently.

In her sleepy state Amanda looked around, then remembered she was Little Dove. "I'm scared," she said before she could stop herself.

The chief frowned. "Why should you be scared? You have strong magic or Raven would have taken you too. You are too important to be scared."

I don't feel any different, important or not, Amanda thought. She felt hungry and irritable. And scared.

The chief led her across the hard earthen floor to the fire and motioned for her to sit with the shaman and others. Amanda knew she should have been honoured to be included in the council, and she would have been, had she not felt so much like Amanda Elizabeth Atkins who was only here because she had to write a report.

The shaman nodded at Amanda. "We will eat before we discuss how to get the women back from Raven," he said.

Five boys appeared, some carrying big carved bowls which looked to Amanda like wooden baby bathtubs, and some carrying bowls made of tightly woven cedar bark. They placed the bowls in front of the shaman and chief. Amanda leaned forward and looked into the bowls. Her hunger vanished. Great blobs of fish in some kind of liquid!

Amanda wished she could get out of there. She wished she'd packed a peanut-butter sandwich. She wished she had some of her chocolates. Fish!

"Eat, Little Dove," the shaman commanded.

Amanda fiddled with the end of her hair. She knew if one piece of that greasy fish touched her lips she would be sick—all over the council members. Suddenly she thought she heard from far off a mocking laugh. Kih-kih-kih. She whirled around. The men looked at her curiously, as though they had heard nothing. Trust the genie to put her in a legend with fish and then laugh!

"Eat, Little Dove. Raven cannot be bested on an empty stomach."

Amanda wondered what happened to Indian children if they didn't eat. They couldn't be sent to their rooms. Maybe they were sent outside, into the forest.

"Little Dove is scared," the chief taunted. "Scared like the bird whose name she bears."

Suddenly Amanda knew what to say. She looked at him with as much pride as she could summon. "I am scared, yes. Scared for my mother and my aunts and sisters whom Raven has kidnapped. I cannot eat fish because it is fish that has made Raven angry with us. We returned the first salmon to the spirit, but we did not give many to Raven. We were afraid there would not be enough for us, and we thought we were more important than Raven. Besides, we were tired of his greediness. I will eat no fish until we get our women back." And then, she thought, I can get out of here and get a hamburger. The men looked at her admiringly.

"Wisely spoken, Little Dove. You will be a great council member like your mother," the shaman said. He turned to the boys. "Bring us berries and dried meat."

When the shaman had finished eating he rapped the talking stick sharply on the floor. From the folds of his robe he took a little decorated wooden box which he handed to Amanda.

"You must bathe now and rub yourself with this lotion. It has strong magic in it."

Amanda opened the box. It had a wild, woodsy, summery smell. She was led behind a curtain of cedar bark where a tub of water steamed gently.

She took off her woven dress and stepped in. There was neither soap nor a cloth, but Amanda didn't mind since she didn't think she was particularly dirty. She stepped out onto the bearskin and used the lotion. It was sticky and she was wet so it took a lot of effort to apply.

After she dressed she walked back to the fire. Beside the shaman was a cedar basket decorated with red and black figures and designs. He stood up and placed a wreath of branches around her neck and some twigs in her hair. "Spruce and hemlock to give you power," he said.

Then he led her outside. "You will lay a trail of salmon for Raven, placing the last salmon inside a circle we have made at the end of the trail. Then you will sit inside the circle and wait. Raven will not be able to resist the salmon. When he walks into the circle you must throw this rope over his head." The shaman handed her a coil of woven bark.

"When Raven finds himself caught he will be very angry. He will run around and try to fly. You must not let him." He looked at her sternly and she nodded. "It is very important that you do not talk to Raven until you have the rope on him. Do you understand?" Amanda nodded again and shivered under the strong, hypnotic stare of the shaman.

He handed her the basket. Fish! Tens and hundreds and thousands of slimy, scaly, cold, wet fish!

Solemnly the Indians led her to the beginning of the trail—a narrow path which wound between the huge evergreens, in places speckled with the few sunbeams that struggled through the branches overhead. The men turned and seemed to disappear into the forest.

Amanda looked into the heavy basket. Hundreds of round eyes were staring up at her. Already the salmon had begun to smell.

Ugh! she thought. I can't touch these fish! What am I going to do? She looked around for help. Nothing happened. I guess I *have* to do it. It's the only way to get those women back and to get me home. Ugh!

She closed her eyes and said, "I am not Amanda. I am Little Dove, and Little Dove likes fish." So thinking, she grasped a cold, slimy fish and threw it on the ground. She opened her eyes and shook her hand. "Ugh!" she gagged.

Amanda walked a few steps farther along the trail, the basket heavy and smelly on her shoulder. She closed her eyes, shoved her hand into the basket, and threw another slimy, scaly, smelly fish onto the trail. Some scales stuck to her hand and she tried to scrape them off in the dirt. Fighting nausea, she continued down the trail, the basket getting lighter, her hand getting smellier, saying over and over to herself, I am Little Dove. I am important. Come on, Raven, get your fish.

The last fish. She looked around, suddenly afraid she'd misjudged the distance and would have to go back and move all the fish. But just ahead the trail widened and she could see a circle drawn in the middle of the clearing. Amanda placed the last salmon in the circle and sat down as far away from it as she could. She coiled the rope and held on to one end.

The sun grew hotter and hotter. It beat down on the dust and pebbles. It beat down on Amanda's head. It beat down on the fish, whose smell grew and hovered around her until it seemed almost visible.

At first Amanda tried to forget the fish. She watched the dust motes in the sunlight. She thought about Flame. She thought about her parents, about the genie, even about Cynthia. She stuck her finger into a parade of ants and watched them detour. She tried to plan how she would write her report.

But after an hour the odour of fish became so overpowering that Amanda could think of nothing but getting away. Her legs were crampy and twitchy, her back hurt and her head was beginning to ache. She had an overwhelming desire to stand up, but the shaman had said to sit. This was worse than posing for her mother, and Amanda had thought few things could be worse than that. All she wanted was to finish the legend, to get back to her bedroom and her comfortable bluejeans, to let the genie know what she thought of him for making her touch fish.

She uncrossed her legs and stuck them out in front. That helped a bit. She coiled and uncoiled the rope.

There was a rustling noise up the path and the trees began to sway violently. Amanda sat straighter. Her heart beat hard and the palms of her hands grew wet.

Out of the dark shadows across the trail moved an even darker shadow. Around the curve in the path it came, paused to gulp a fish, then moved toward her, its eyes riveted on the last fish. Raven! Amanda swallowed hard. She had expected a bird like a crow, or maybe like an eagle, but not this! This was the biggest bird she had ever seen! Bigger than the emus in the zoo, bigger than the bears in the zoo! As big as Hyak the killer whale!

Raven half waddled, half loped into the circle and gulped the last fish. Then he noticed her. "Is that all?" he croaked.

Amanda stared. She was too frightened to do anything else.

"Is that all the fish?"

She nodded.

"Then I'll be off ... or should I eat you too?" He flapped his wings menacingly and stuck out his head.

Quickly Amanda threw the rope over Raven's neck. She scrambled to her feet and pulled. "Got you!"

"Why should you want to get me? I was just walking along minding my own business. Found some fish so I ate them." He sounded hurt and pathetic, yet his eyes darted from side to side looking for an escape.

"I am Little Dove. I have great magic. You could not capture me when you took my mother and sisters. Now you must tell me where they are." Amanda was· pleased with how convincing she sounded.

"A trap, is it? All right, you win. Take this rope off and I'll bring them back." He looked at her from the corner of his eye.

Amanda did not trust him. "No. I'd better come with you, then I'll know they're all right."

"You can trust me," Raven croaked in an injured tone.

"I don't know that," Amanda replied. "And I have to get them back or I can't go home!" Oh oh, she thought, that was a slip.

But Raven didn't seem to notice. "You'll have to walk. I can't fly with this rope on."

"You'd only fly away if I took the rope off!"

"Who, me? You don't think I'd do a thing like that?"

Amanda didn't bother to reply. "I'll take the rope off, Raven, but you carry me. One false move and it goes back on!"

Raven shrugged his shoulders as if the rope was painful, and looked disgusted.

Amanda climbed onto his back. Only then did she loosen the rope and slip it over his head. Immediately Raven pushed back with his powerful wings. Amanda curled her arms around his neck and hung on. Higher and higher the giant bird soared, over the tops of the huge Douglas firs, over rivers and inlets that looked like pieces of broken mirror, over snowy mountain peaks. The sun looked hotter and the wind felt colder the higher the bird climbed. Amanda was terrified and exhilarated. She buried her head in his feathers and dug her knees into his sides.

Abruptly Raven went into a dive and the wind rushed past. Just as suddenly he reversed and Amanda thought she would fall off the other way. Tail down, head up, Raven began to slow. Amanda noticed a little clearing ahead. She could see the women and girls. They ran up when they saw Raven had a passenger.

"Little Dove! He got you too!"

"I got him!" Amanda slid off Raven's back and walked toward the women. Suddenly she turned back. Raven was flapping his wings, about to take off. Amanda threw the rope, which curved high in the air and settled around his neck.

"You take us all back now," Amanda ordered.

"I can't take you all at once!" Raven said.

"You got them here all at once, didn't you?"

"Poor Raven," Raven muttered. "It's not fair."

"If you'd stop playing tricks," one of the older women said, "you could be our friend."

"You wouldn't give poor Raven any salmon if he didn't trick you."

"That's not true. We share with you what we have. You're just greedy."

Amanda mounted Raven's back first so she could loosen the rope, and the others began to climb on behind her. Then Amanda was really aware of the magic of legends, for Raven's size was increasing to accommodate all the people. He looked like a small airplane. The ride back was even more dizzying and terrifying than before.

Raven landed in the clearing where Amanda had first waited for him, and as everyone climbed down and he returned to what Amanda supposed was his normal size, the men rushed out of the forest and greeted the women.

The chief spoke with Raven and promised him a regular share of their salmon, and Raven promised never to play such a trick again, but to use his power to protect the tribe. The chief said the tribe would adopt Raven as its totem and carve masks in his honour. Raven was so pleased he plumped out his feathers, and with a nod to Amanda, flew away.

The chief turned to Amanda. "Little Dove, you have great magic and have done a brave deed. When you are fully grown you will be trained as a shaman. Now we will have feasting and dancing to honour you and to welcome back the women."

Amanda blushed with embarrassment and pride. She was just about to say, "Thank you, it was nothing really," when she had a funny feeling in her stomach. She closed her eyes.

When she opened them again she was standing in her bedroom dressed in her jeans, her glasses securely on her nose, holding the tube of toothpaste in her hand.

The genie bobbed in his bubble and took his pipe out of his mouth. "Did you have a nice time?"

"It was fine, but you didn't have to bring me back so soon. I wanted to stay for the dancing."

"You would have had to eat the fish this time."

"Speaking of fish—Did you *have* to put me in a legend with them!"

"I've never seen anything so funny as you trying to pick up that first fish!" He doubled over with laughter.

"It wasn't that funny! I think you did it on purpose!"

"Really, Amanda, you are a most ungrateful child!" The genie's laughter subsided into giggles. "I can't pick and choose—well, not much."

"Where was the real Little Dove? Where did she go while I was there and is she back now? What's she like?"

"I don't know, I'm just an apprentice. I suppose she came back. Anyway, I thought you had a report to do. Goodbye."

Amanda turned in her report next morning. It was the longest in the class. When Mrs. Hayward handed them back she called Amanda to her desk. "I gave you an 'A' because you worked so hard. But," she added sternly, "in a report, stick to facts. You must not let your imagination run away with you."

"Yes, Mrs. Hayward," Amanda said politely.

8

That's some horse

One week later Amanda still had not wished for a horse or a baby sister. After her attempt to get ten wishes a day she'd had to use up wishes correcting problems from Monday's wish.

At first she was delighted to have neat hair that stayed together down her back, hair that had no snarls or tangles to be combed out every morning. It was all quite convenient—until her mother told her to wash it. When she lay down in the tub her hair stuck straight out and the shampoo ran right off it as if it were metal in a carwash. Amanda thought that was an improvement over the usual tangly hair-washing, but then her mother came in to help.

Mrs. Atkins picked up Amanda's hair to rinse it, but when she let go, it clanked against Amanda's shoulders. Mrs. Atkins rolled up her sleeves and began scrubbing. She tried hot water. She tried cold water. She even tried rubbing alcohol, thinking the hair was full of gum. Amanda's scalp got very sore and red and Amanda screamed and cried.

The next day she wished her hair to go back to normal. Putting up with snarls and tangles didn't seem so horrible, and at least she could twirl her hair. Now that she could no longer bite her nails—or rather, now she could only bite her nails longer—she seemed to be always needing something to do with her hands. Still, it was the waste of a perfectly good wish.

Amanda had had to waste the next day's wish as well. She was a very restless sleeper and before she became neat her sheets would be completely un-tucked each morning and the blankets on the floor. Frequently her feet stuck out the bottom no matter how firmly the bed was made and once she'd even woken up like Pippi Longstocking, head where her feet should be and toes under the pillow. But after nights of trying to get comfortable with covers that, no matter how much she wriggled, stayed so tucked in she could hardly breathe, she ordered the genie to put her bed back the way it was.

The genie sulked; he didn't like undoing wishes. But Amanda said, "Anyone who can sleep in a toothpaste tube doesn't understand the comfort of a bed," so the genie returned her bed to its messy but comfortable state.

Saturday morning when Amanda woke up she

knew it was the day to wish The Wish. She jumped out of bed, threw on her clothes and grabbed the toothpaste tube. She started to undo the orange cap, but she had only twisted it half a turn before the cap twisted the other way. She tried again, faster. The cap did itself back up. Again Amanda twisted it to the right. But the minute she took her fingers off the cap it twisted to the left until it was as firmly in place as before.

"Now, look!" Amanda shouted. "I know you're in there. Come out! This is really important."

Silence. The cap was as resistant as if it was the top of an old tube of glue. She clamped her left hand firmly on the cap, then twisted the tube around and around in her right. Sluggishly the tube parted from its lid. Slowly, ever so slowly, hardly-as-noticeably-as-a-snail slowly, the purple bubble began to form. Amanda squeezed harder.

"OUCH! You don't have to be violent!" The genie peered at her through half-closed eyes. "I was still asleep."

"You weren't going to come out!"

"It's only seven o'clock. And it's Saturday. Don't you ever sleep in?"

"Are all genies as grumpy as you?"

"I'm not grumpy!" he grumbled. "Well, let's have it. What wish do you want me to change now? Each time you make me undo one I have to leave it out of my report. Soon I won't have a thing left to include."

"I want a whole new wish today."

"That's better." He sat up and yawned. "But *I* wish you could wait till a reasonable hour."

"This is a reasonable hour. I want a horse."

"A horse?"

"Yes, a horse. You know, a horse."

"I do? I know a horse?"

"What's with you? Everyone knows what a horse is. Four legs and a mane and tail. You ride them."

"I'm not *everyone*. I'm *me*." The genie rubbed his eyes and yawned again. Amanda wasn't sure if he really didn't know what a horse was or if he was pretending to be stupid because it was early. But he said, "Sounds like the sort of wish the Master Genie likes," so she felt relieved.

"I want Flame," she said.

"But you said you wanted a horse." The genie looked genuinely puzzled.

"I want a horse like Flame."

"Jumping Geniacs, Amanda. I can't do that."

"Why not?"

"You didn't say 'I wish.'"

"*I wish* you'd make me a horse like Flame. Please."

"Still can't."

"Oh, come on. Why not now?"

"I don't know what a 'Flame' horse looks like."

"Oh, is that all? Flame is a stallion the colour of his name. He's huge—really huge. And fierce. He won't let anyone ride him but me and with me he's as gentle as a lamb."

"Okay, there you go," the genie said.

As Amanda watched, her anticipation changed to fear. In the far corner of her bedroom was an animal so tall its ears brushed the ceiling. It was covered with red and gold spots and with each breath fire sprang from its nostrils. It might have been a dragon for all Amanda knew. It certainly wasn't a horse.

When it caught sight of her crouching behind the closet door it gave a snort of recognition that singed the bedspread and started towards her. She wanted to close herself in the closet but she was so scared her hands slipped on the doorknob. The thing tripped over the desk leg, stomped on her doll house, then laid its head on Amanda's knee and immediately changed into a sort of giant lamb.

The thing's affectionate nuzzling pressed wads of smelly wool into her mouth and nostrils until Amanda thought she was going to suffocate. With difficulty she managed to turn her head sideways. In her hand was the toothpaste tube with an extremely small bubble at the top. She could see the genie staring at his creation.

"Make it go away!" Amanda screamed through the wool.

"I think it's very good." The genie's voice was as tiny as his bubble. "We're graded on size and originality."

"I don't care. It's going to kill me!"

"No, no, it's gentle as a lamb with you, remember?"

Amanda was desperate. The thing was pressing against her so firmly she'd lost the feeling in her legs. Now it began to rub its head up and down her chest, but it was so strong it only succeeded in rubbing her up and down the wall.

"If my mum comes in you'll get it," Amanda gasped. "She'll make you pose."

The genie's size increased a little and he peered at her anxiously. "Do you think she would?"

"I'm positive! And if she doesn't I'll take the cap off every hour and squeeze your tube so you'll never get any sleep!"

"Oh, all right, but it's the most sensational thing I've done."

Amanda collapsed with relief as the thing vanished. She was lying there catching her breath when she saw that the genie's bubble was disappearing. "Oh, no, you don't!" She squeezed the tube angrily. "I still don't have my horse!"

The genie popped back up. "What do you mean?

I've granted your wish for the day. As a matter of fact, I've granted two. And I can't even put it in my report!" He looked as if he would cry.

"Why not?"

"We can't take credit for something that would harm our owners," he quoted. "And I guess that animal could have killed you with kindness."

"It's too bad you can't put it in your report. It *was* pretty fantastic." Amanda smiled. "But you could take credit for a real horse, couldn't you?"

"I suppose so," the genie replied sulkily, "but that's commonplace. And I did give you exactly what you described!"

"You know I meant one I could ride!"

"No, I didn't. Anyway, there's no point talking about it. That's your wish for today."

"*No!*" Amanda shouted to keep him from disappearing. "It's not my wish if you can't put it in your report."

The genie looked at her. "But it says just one on my label. I didn't write the label. That's the rules. And I'm getting sleepy. We need a lot of sleep, you know."

"I know, I know. You keep telling me. But you also need something to put in your report. Why don't we start all over again?"

The genie sucked on his pipe, which had gone out. He stared at it, then very slowly and deliberately flicked his finger and thumb together to produce a light. Amanda forgot and bit her fingernail. She watched as it grew.

"We—ll,"—the genie dragged out the word as though it were the biggest *well* in the world—"I guess if I can't report it, it doesn't count."

"Whew," Amanda sighed.

"But I gave you exactly what you described. You'll have to be more accurate."

"Can't you read minds? I thought you said genies could."

The genie looked embarrassed. "Apprentices aren't supposed to. That's for when we graduate. But I do know how," he admitted.

Amanda smiled, and he smiled back. It was the first time he had smiled directly at her, the first time they had shared a smile. His was rather sly, but still, a smile was a smile.

"I'll make a picture of Flame in my mind and you can copy him, okay?"

The genie nodded.

Amanda scrunched her eyes up and thought of Flame as clearly as she could. Suddenly her eyes snapped open. "Don't make him here—"

But it was too late. The genie had disappeared.

Then Amanda forgot everything in the thrill of looking at her horse. He stood in the middle of the room, definitely chestnut, definitely a stallion, with a noble head and ears pricked forward, with deep, warm, dark brown, intelligent eyes watching her. He was wearing an English saddle and bridle.

"Oh, Flame."

He whinnied in reply. Amanda stood beside him, patting his neck while he nuzzled her pockets. He was exactly the right horse. "Thank you, you marvellous genie," she whispered.

"Amanda! Come for breakfast!"

Flame started. Amanda put her hand over his nose in case he decided to whinny again.

"Amanda!"

"Coming!" What am I going to do? she thought, stepping into the hall and closing the bedroom door tightly. Then she opened it again. Maybe while her parents were eating would be the best time to get Flame out of the house. But from the kitchen table they could see into the back yard. And she couldn't leave him in the front of the house; he might wander down the road or a neighbour might see him. She closed the door again. Maybe she would have a better chance of getting him out of the house after breakfast. Sometimes her parents went shopping on Saturdays. Why hadn't the genie made Flame appear outside?

"*Amanda!*"

"Coming!" Move him now or later? It was too

late. Mrs. Atkins was at the end of the hall. Flame would have to stay in the bedroom until she could think of some way to get him out.

9
The phony!

"I was just coming." Amanda scooted into her place so fast she knocked over her glass of milk. "Sorry," she said, getting the dishcloth.

Her parents looked at each other, then started to laugh. "That's more like the old Amanda," her father chuckled. "You've been pretty strange all week. It's nice to see you can do something normal."

Amanda stood still, not sure whether that was a compliment or not. But at least her parents weren't angry with her.

Suddenly there was a terrific noise from the direction of her bedroom. "What was that?" her mother asked.

Amanda swung around and the cloth in her hand sent the jug of pancake syrup crashing to the floor.

"Now look what you've done!" her father said, grabbing the cloth.

"What was that noise?" Mrs. Atkins repeated.

"Um, must have been some books."

"Sounded like the whole library," her father said.

Amanda stuffed some pancake into her mouth. If only she could get back to Flame before he decided to whinny.

"Stop eating and clean up that mess," Mr. Atkins ordered. "Once is an accident, but twice is a mess!"

"All right," Amanda said, taking the cloth.

"Not that way!" This time her mother grabbed the cloth. "I'd better do it. You just eat."

"She should clean up her own messes," her father began.

Amanda had so much pancake in her mouth she couldn't chew. Maybe her parents would argue and she could get Flame outside.

"She'll just make more mess," Mrs. Atkins said.

"I suppose so." Mr. Atkins went into the living room, the newspaper under his arm.

"I'm finished, Mum," Amanda said. Even if her parents weren't going to have an argument, it would be her only chance to move Flame before he gave everything away. Her father's favourite chair faced away from the hall, and her mother was getting ready to wash the kitchen floor. But just then there was a whinny. Abruptly Amanda opened her mouth and bellowed, "Whewhewheee."

Mrs. Atkins jumped. "What was that for?"

"I'm a horse." Amanda cantered twice around the kitchen, then galloped through the living room and down the hall to her bedroom.

Flame had knocked over the chair to her desk. When Amanda opened the door he looked up and his leg became stuck in the chair rungs. He clattered backwards into the bookcase, snorting with fear and making the most awful noise.

"Whoa, boy," Amanda said soothingly, and as he quieted she lifted the chair away from his leg. Quickly she gathered the reins and stuck her head out the door to see if the way was clear.

Just then Mr. Atkins shouted from the living room, "You do sound convincing, Amanda. I'd almost swear you had a real horse in there!"

"I'm getting better at it!" she shouted back, then quietly to Flame, "Come on." She tugged his reins and started down the hall to the den, whinnying again to cover up the noise Flame's hoofs made even on the carpet. "Thank heaven my bedroom's not upstairs," she thought.

Suddenly Amanda pulled the horse into the bathroom, crashed the door shut and turned the lock. Not any too soon, for her mother was also heading for the bathroom.

"Really, Amanda," Mrs. Atkins said, "if you're going to be a horse, will you please go outside. Horses don't belong in houses. I can't think with all that clattering! What *do* you have on your feet?"

"Sorry!" Amanda yelled. Flame had managed to wedge himself sideways between the sink and the bathtub. She pushed his flank and pulled on the bridle. "I'm just getting ready to go out!" Amanda held her breath and put her hand over Flame's nostrils in case he decided to join in the conversation.

"Are you sure you're all right?" Mrs. Atkins tried the doorknob.

"I'm fine—oof!" Flame had butted her with his head.

Amanda waited a little longer. Finally she heard her mother going back to the kitchen. She waited another few minutes, then quietly slipped open the door. The den was just a few more paces down the hall. She started to lead Flame out, then she sniffed. The essence of horse was overpowering. The bathroom smelled distinctly like a stable. Amanda got out the can of air-freshener and sprayed. At least now it smelled like a stable in a pine forest.

Holding Flame firmly by the bridle she led him into the den and through the sliding glass door onto the patio. Then she pulled him around the side of the house before her mother could look out the window. Flame began to eat the grass. She tied him securely to the fence.

Amanda dashed into the kitchen and plowed straight into her mother. "Oof!" they both said. "Do slow down," Mrs. Atkins added.

Amanda yanked open the crisper of the fridge and took out two carrots. Mrs. Atkins' eyebrows went way up. "I thought you hated carrots."

"Horses don't. Besides, you keep telling me to try

different food." She jiggled the crisper impatiently. It always stuck. "Are you and Daddy going out soon?"

"I don't think so. Why?"

"Just wondered. Oh well, bye." She dashed down the hall, through the den door and outside. Flame looked up, a purple petunia dangling from his mouth. "Oh no, bad horse. You're only supposed to eat the grass."

Flame had already enlivened his diet with the new row of petunias Mrs. Atkins had planted only ten days before. He had left three plants he couldn't reach and a pile of fresh manure in return. Amanda kicked some dirt over the manure, hoping it wouldn't be noticed.

How to get Flame out of the back yard was still a problem. Her mother might look out the kitchen window and see him. It was too bad, Amanda thought, that all the big trees in the yard grew right against the fence. There was no room to hide behind them.

Amanda left Flame and crept along the side of the house until she was under the kitchen window. She peeked in. Her mother was wiping the counter. But the coffee pot was steaming; that was a good sign. Amanda settled back, absentmindedly pulled a carrot from her pocket and took a bite. It wasn't as bad as she had remembered. A moment later she peeked again. There! Mrs. Atkins was pouring the coffee. Amanda hoped she'd take it into the living room as she usually did.

She ran back to Flame, untied him and without looking at the house because that might be bad luck trotted him over to the gate and into the lane.

The palms of her hands were sweating. She wiped them on her jeans and bit her lip, thinking that Flame was a very tall horse. Then he turned his head and looked at her as if to say, "Aren't we ever going to get going?" She moved him around so she was on a piece of higher ground, slid the reins over his head and put her foot in the stirrup. She grabbed the front of the saddle and scrambled up. Flame stood very still until she was ready.

"Okay, boy, let's go." She squeezed her legs against his sides and he moved up the lane at a sedate walk. From the saddle Amanda could see over the high fences which bordered the lane and into the back yards. In one, three small boys were digging in a pile of dirt. Between the houses she caught glimpses of the mountains and the blue sparkle of Burrard Inlet. It was much more interesting to ride up the lane than to walk.

Amanda patted Flame's neck. He chewed his bit and danced for a few steps in response, but very carefully, as if he felt responsible for his rider.

In the last yard on the block Amanda saw Cynthia playing ball with her little sister. Just as Amanda drew level with their yard, Cynthia looked up. Her mouth fell open and her eyes grew huge. She dropped the ball and ran over.

"Hey, where'd you get the horse?"

Amanda shrugged. "Just got him."

"Oh yeah? Your parents wouldn't buy you a horse! And anyway, where are you keeping it?"

"It's none of your business where I got him and likewise none of your business where I keep him!"

Cynthia, paying no attention to Amanda's outburst, climbed over her gate. "Can I have a ride?"

"Nope, he won't let anyone ride him but *me*, and anyway, we have to go now."

When Amanda looked back Cynthia was still standing in the middle of the lane with her mouth gaping foolishly. Amanda laughed and patted Flame's neck.

She continued up the back lanes until they came to the high school. When they reached the grass she gave Flame his head. He jumped from a walk to a gallop and tore around the perimeter of the field, scattering clumps of sod and Saturday morning ball players. His gait was so smooth it was like riding the wind. His hoofs hardly touched the grass and Amanda could almost sit completely still in the saddle. Round and round they went, and she laughed in delight. It was unlike anything she'd ever experienced. She thought that together she and Flame could do anything in the whole world.

When they'd circled the field three times Amanda pulled Flame down to a trot, then a walk. He was hardly even warm. He snorted and pranced as though he wanted to go on forever.

"Get that horse off the school grounds! Horses aren't allowed!" A man with a baseball cap and a catcher's mitt ran up, red in the face and yelling. He was followed by the rest of the team. Amanda recognized some of the players; they were in her class. "This field's reserved for the Little League—not the equestrian Olympics! Now get that horse outa here! Look what you've done to the grass!"

Amanda's wonderful feeling dissolved and was replaced by a knot in her stomach. She looked behind her. Flame's hoofs had torn great chunks out of the smooth field.

"Hey, Amanda, is that your horse?" Jason asked.

She nodded. She and Flame were surrounded by ball players, all trying to stroke Flame.

"Wow," Peter said, "that's sure some horse."

"You take him up to the bridle paths in the university grounds," the coach said less angrily. "Come on, team, let's get back to our practice."

Amanda walked Flame out of the high school yard and up Sixteenth Avenue, past her own school and the oval track. The forest started there, separating the university from the city. The woods were riddled with paths.

She squeezed Flame into a trot and felt happier. Paths with trees hanging over them and the occasional log to jump were better than a school field, anyway.

Flame whinnied and stopped so suddenly that Amanda was thrown forward onto his neck. Around a bend in the path came a man wearing a riding helmet, breeches and boots.

"There you are, you devil," he said.

Flame pricked up his ears and blew gently.

"Where did you find him?" the man asked Amanda. "He bucked me off and ran away a couple of hours ago. He's a real handful. I was afraid he'd get into the streets and be hurt—he's not used to traffic."

Amanda was too shocked to say anything.

The man took the reins and stroked the horse's neck. "My name's Jim Sutherland, by the way," he added. "I'm so glad you found him. Thank you very much."

Amanda stared at the ground and blinked hard. She wasn't going to cry in front of this man, she told herself.

"You can get down now," Mr. Sutherland said after a moment.

Dumbly Amanda slid out of the saddle. She reached her hand toward Flame's neck, then withdrew it.

The man was staring at her. "The more I think about it, the stranger it gets. Flame's a real devil. I've never found anyone who could handle him, let alone a child. You must be some horsewoman. Where did you learn to ride like that?"

Amanda shrugged.

"Well, thanks again." He gathered up the reins and vaulted into the saddle. Flame half reared and gave a few bucks. Then he turned his head to Amanda and whickered softly. Mr. Sutherland wheeled him around and cantered down the path.

Amanda watched until they disappeared, then turned the other way. She couldn't hold back the tears any longer. "It's not fair. He was *my* horse. The genie made him and I was the only one who could ride him. It's not fair." She shoved her hands in her pockets. Her glasses were so fogged from her tears she couldn't see where she was going and tripped over a rock.

"How could he do that to me? It's not fair giving me someone else's horse. He's just a great big phony!" She picked up the rock and threw it hard against a tree. "I'm going to cut his toothpaste tube in half! What a mean, dirty trick! The phony!" She heard hoofbeats behind her, but paid no attention.

"Wait up!" It was the man and Flame again. Amanda didn't care.

"I wasn't thinking straight," he said, slowing Flame to a walk. The horse butted Amanda's back and in spite of her misery she turned and gave him the carrot still in her pocket.

"You get along with Flame so well, won't you come and ride him for me sometimes? He needs more exercise than I can give him and I often have to go out of town on business. Flame and I could use you."

Amanda looked up. The man was smiling expectantly.

She nodded. At least she could ride Flame. She could pretend he was hers. It was the next best thing to owning him herself.

"I'd like that, thank you." She leaned her head on Flame's shoulder and he turned to nuzzle her.

"Here's my phone number and address and where Flame's stable is." He scribbled on a piece of paper and handed it to her. "Have your parents phone me tonight. Between us, we'll talk them into letting you exercise Flame, won't we?"

Amanda carefully folded the paper. "We sure will."

She watched the man and Flame canter away again. But this time she knew it wasn't forever. She felt a little happier, although underneath that happiness she was still very angry with the genie.

The minute she got home she stormed down the hall, slammed her bedroom door and hauled out the toothpaste tube. When the bubble had grown and she could make out the genie she shouted, "It was *mean* of you to give me Flame and then take him away like that! I wanted him all to myself!"

"Aren't we selfish," the genie replied in a smirky, sulky sort of tone. "You have a horse to ride. What more do you want?"

"I wanted my very own horse!"

"I can't make something out of nothing, you know!" The genie took four fast puffs on his pipe and the smoke swirled around him.

"You made the first horse out of nothing!"

"That was just make-believe. It didn't count! And it was stupid of you to ride right smack into Flame's owner!"

"You *stole* Flame!"

"Are you calling me a thief?" The bubble began to froth.

"Yes I am! You took him away from his owner and gave him to me and *that's stealing*!" Then, in spite of her anger, her mouth twitched into a smile. She had had a sudden mental picture of the genie grabbing Flame out from under a surprised Mr. Sutherland and plunking him in her bedroom.

But the genie met Amanda's anger with his own. "I have to grant your wishes. If you're going to wish for something like a horse I have to produce it the best way I can!" He scratched his green hair. "Besides, this works out pretty well. I mean, where were you going to keep a horse—in the garage? And how were you going to feed it and how were you going to explain it to your parents? Didn't think of that, did you? This way you don't have those problems." His bubble had calmed down and he puffed at his pipe. "No, I think this is a better solution. Not too startling for my report, but what do you expect from a little kid?"

"I'm not little!" Amanda replied. But she could see the logic of his statements. Telling her parents she'd acquired a horse would have been a problem. And now she did have a horse—well, half a horse.

"Okay, genie," Amanda relented, "we'll leave it at that for now. But next time you'd better make sure you grant my wish so I'll be able to keep it!"

The genie yawned, nodded and shrank back into the tube.

10
The BIG wish

It was a number of days before Amanda talked with the genie again. For one thing there were practices for Sports Day after school, and for another there was Flame to be ridden. On the weekend both Amanda and her father had helped Mrs. Atkins transport her paintings to the Art Gallery for her show.

But all the time Amanda was doing these things she was thinking about how to get the genie to grant her most important wish without turning it into a mess or a practical joke the way he usually did. Finally she thought she had the answer.

She dug out the familiar purple and green tube and undid the orange cap. She squeezed, gently at first, then harder, her fingers working their way up from the end of the tube. There was hardly any toothpaste left. Even when the purple bubble was fully formed it seemed smaller than it had been at first. The genie was in his most sulky and difficult mood, but Amanda didn't care. She had her plan all figured out.

"Genie, you told me you can't make something out of nothing. Is that true?"

"Can't seem to make anything. I'm a failure as a genie."

"No you're not," Amanda replied automatically. "But you can't make something out of nothing so you need something to start with, right?"

The genie nodded. He hadn't even lit his pipe today.

Amanda took a deep breath. "Can you make something come alive if it isn't alive in the first place?" This was the most important part of her plan. If she just asked the genie for a baby sister he might produce one the way he had Flame, and that would be kidnapping.

"I suppose I can make something come alive, but I'll probably just foul it up somehow."

"What's the matter?"

"Nothing."

Amanda looked at the genie. His round cheeks had sunk into ovals. He seemed smaller than usual and the purple of his bubble wasn't so bright.

"Don't worry about me," he sighed. "I'm only here to grant your wishes. Doesn't matter what happens to me."

"You're just feeling sorry for yourself. Come on, tell me."

The genie rolled his pipe stem around in his mouth. Two tears gathered in the corners of his eyes and began a slow journey down his face. He mumbled something.

"What did you say?"

"I said I'm not going to graduate! Not that it matters . . . I'm just a failure."

"How do you know you won't graduate?"

"I just know. I don't have enough for my report. I'll be the only one not to graduate and I'll have to be an apprentice again. And it's all your fault!"

"My fault?"

"If you'd only wished for something proper—but you wished for stupid things—making a fish disappear, talking to a cat, getting a box of chocolates and a horse—even then I couldn't use the unusual one I'd created. And being neat! That was even more difficult, especially in your case."

Amanda just sat, her mouth open in astonishment.

"Course I knew that's what would happen when I had a little kid for an owner!"

Suddenly Amanda found her voice. "Don't you blame me! Everything I wished for you goofed up! You *like* getting me into trouble. I only wished for what I wanted, and then you wouldn't grant it—like my ten wishes a day! And you *said* you could put the candies and Flame in your report! But you made the horse appear in my bedroom so I nearly got into trouble and you made me neat so fast everyone was suspicious and you made me talk *French* and you made the fish disappear just about in front of my mother! I think you hate me and want me to get into trouble! And anyway, *I am not little*!"

The genie's anger faded under Amanda's attack. He started to cry again. "You're right. Absolutely right. I *have* goofed everything up—it was more fun that way. But now it's too late. If I don't graduate I have to go into another toothpaste tube or even worse, a box of soap powder. That makes me sneeze."

"But you're a genie. Why don't *you* wish you could graduate?"

"You don't understand," he replied self-pityingly.

Amanda pressed her lips together trying to control her temper. "No, I don't understand. Why don't you tell me?"

"I'm a genie. I have no power of my own. I can only do what my owner wants. And fulfilling wishes is all that counts in my report. If my owner doesn't wish for things the Master Genie approves of and I can't perform them, I don't graduate. It's very simple."

"He must be a dumb Master Genie. It shouldn't be your fault if your owner doesn't wish for things he likes. You should be judged on how well you do what is asked of you."

"That's what I think too. But the Master doesn't and he's in charge." The genie sat shrivelled up in his bubble, his pipe forgotten in his lap.

Amanda got up and walked around the room. She stared out the window and chewed the end of her hair. "If you graduate, I won't have you any more?"

"You won't have me whether I do or not. Once this toothpaste is used up I either graduate or go back on the shelf."

"How much time do you have left?"

"We have to give our reports tomorrow. There isn't enough time. I shouldn't have fooled around so much." He started to cry again.

"Stop blubbering and let me think!"

The genie busied himself with his pipe, but it was too wet to light.

"What sort of wishes does the Master Genie like you to grant?"

"He likes things," the genie replied despondently. "Big mansions, gorgeous clothes. Producing a roomful of jewels is a sure way to graduate."

"He sounds pretty old-fashioned," Amanda observed. "I can just see my parents if I wished for a roomful of jewels."

"See what I mean?"

"Hey, can *I* wish for you to graduate?"

"Oh, no! That would just get me into more trouble! I'm not even supposed to have mentioned this. Discussing personal problems with one's owner is forbidden—page 33 in the manual, underlined twice."

"Oh—well, would it only take one wish?"

"One proper sort of wish. I guess I can build up the horse and legend and candy wishes and explain about being owned by a child . . . "

Amanda glared at him, then "There's enough time. I think we can work it out."

The genie looked at her hopefully.

"Okay," she said with finality, "you grant my wish today with no jokes and see that nothing goes wrong, and tomorrow I'll wish the sort of wish that'll make sure you graduate. But you have to give me a baby sister and you can't just steal her, okay?"

"Okay."

"No jokes?"

"No jokes."

"You're sure you can't make her out of nothing?"

"Only money."

"What?"

"Money is the only thing I can make out of nothing. Governments do it all the time."

"I said no jokes!"

"Sorry."

"But you can make something come alive?"

"Depends what it is."

Amanda reached into her closet and pulled out a large, soft-bodied doll. It had no eyelashes and its hair was matted and worn. "Can you use this to make me a baby sister?"

The genie examined it. "It'd be easier to get you a baby from a nursery."

"No way! That's kidnapping, and the parents would be really sad! I don't think you have any feelings!"

"I have genie feelings, not people feelings!"

"Anyway, if you could make a baby out of this doll then she'd be ours and no one could take her away."

"If that's what you want, then it's done." The doll vanished.

Amanda looked around suspiciously. "Where'd you put her?"

"I put her on the doorstep. Isn't that where babies come from? And—Amanda"—his face turned a darker purple—"I'm sorry for the jokes I've played. You're really not so bad for a lit— for a k— not so bad." He smiled a very wide open friendly smile.

Amanda smiled back. She suddenly realized she was going to miss him. "You go to sleep now and don't worry. I'll think of some way to wish a wish the Master Genie would like."

The genie continued to smile as he shrank into the tube.

11
It's out of the question

The doorbell rang. Amanda ran into the living room just as her father peered out the door and said, "That's funny. There's no one there."

Before he could sit down the bell rang again. Mr. Atkins opened the door wide. "Darn kids, ringing doorbells and running away," he muttered. He started to close the door, but heard a faint noise like a kitten mewing and looked down. "Oh, no," he moaned.

There on the doorstep in an old-fashioned wicker laundry basket was a bundle of pink blankets. The blankets twitched, and out of them came another little cry.

"Omigosh," said Mrs. Atkins.

"It's a baby." Amanda started to pick it up.

"Just a minute," her father said. "I'll bring the whole thing in. Do you know anything about this, Amanda?"

"It's a baby," she repeated.

"I can see it's a baby. The question is, whose baby?"

"It's our baby. Isn't she cute?" Amanda pulled the blankets away from the baby's face and the first thing she saw was the baby's hair, matted and patchy and blonde just like the doll's. She grabbed the pink blankets out of the basket and laid them on the chesterfield.

"Amanda!" her mother said. "Be careful. You can't throw a baby around like a doll!"

Amanda ignored her. She had to find out if it was a real baby. Maybe the genie had only made the doll able to move and cry like a baby. She pulled the blankets farther down and freed the baby's arm, felt it from shoulder to hand, then moved it around. The arm was warm and it bent at the elbow and wrist, unlike the doll's, which had only flopped from the shoulder. When Amanda felt the baby's fist it opened and the baby grabbed her fingers.

"A real baby," Amanda breathed. "Our real baby."

"*Our* baby?" Mr. and Mrs. Atkins said together. "What do you mean, *our* baby?"

Amanda looked up. She looked at the baby. She looked around the room. She giggled nervously. "I mean, it was on our doorstep so it must be ours." She smiled at her parents. Her parents frowned at her.

The baby's whimpers accelerated into serious

complaints. Mrs. Atkins picked her up and patted her back. Mr. Atkins sifted through the blankets. "There might be a note. Some poor deranged person might have left it . . . No, there's no note, but here's a bottle."

That was nice of the genie, Amanda thought.

"I'll warm it up. The poor thing's probably hungry," Mrs. Atkins said. "Here, Amanda, you hold her."

Amanda sat down, settled the baby comfortably in her lap and pulled the blankets back some more. The baby's face screwed up. She gave a couple of little cries and waved her fists around. One fist hit her cheek; she turned her head and began to suck her fingers.

"Our very own baby," Amanda repeated. "Isn't she cute, Mum? Dad?"

"She's a regular little doll," Mr. Atkins said, leaning over her.

Amanda looked at him, startled, afraid he'd somehow found out. Then she said, "Let's call her Sarah, okay?"

"Now just hang on. She's not our baby. I'm going out to see if whoever left her is nearby." He banged out the front door.

"You won't find anyone," Amanda shouted, then bit her tongue.

Mrs. Atkins came back with the bottle and took

the baby. Amanda pried the baby's fist out of her mouth and just as the baby started to yell Mrs. Atkins popped the nipple in. The baby began to suck and slurp and gulp, breathing noisily at the same time.

"She sure doesn't have any manners," Amanda observed.

"She acts as if she's never been fed before," Mrs. Atkins said.

I guess that's true enough, Amanda thought. "We can keep her, can't we, Mum? She can share my room and I'll look after her."

"Don't be silly," Mrs. Atkins said sharply. "Of course we can't keep her. She belongs to someone else. We'll have to phone the police so they can find her parents."

"But she was left for *us*! We must keep her!"

Was this another of the genie's jokes in spite of his promise? Was he keeping his part of the bargain only to have Amanda's parents give Sarah up?

Mrs. Atkins rubbed the baby's back. The baby burped loudly and dribbled milk on Mrs. Atkins' sleeve. "That's better, isn't it?" she crooned. As she wiped her sleeve she said, "See if there's a diaper in the basket, Amanda."

"I'm calling her Sarah anyway," Amanda said, locating a diaper and handing it to her mother.

Mrs. Atkins laid Sarah on the couch and proceeded to change her diaper. "Look at her lovely skin! But what a funny birthmark!"

Amanda looked at the faint red line on the baby's tummy. Then she remembered. Once she'd played hospital with the doll as patient and had drawn a scar on its stomach with lipstick. She'd tried to scrub it off afterwards, but hadn't been successful. When the genie had changed the doll into a real baby he had forgotten about the mark.

"If the police can't find her parents then we can keep her, can't we?" Amanda demanded.

"Oh, no. If her real parents can't look after her then a social worker will find a family who want to adopt her."

Amanda felt this was getting too complicated. "But *we* want to adopt her," she insisted.

Mrs. Atkins gave her a peculiar look, but just then Mr. Atkins came back.

"I couldn't see anyone," he reported, slamming the front door.

Sarah jumped and began to cry.

Mr. Atkins picked her up. "My, you are a big girl, aren't you, you teeny weeny sweetie-pie," he comforted in a special talk-to-babies voice.

Mrs. Atkins went into the kitchen to phone the police.

"Please, Dad, let's adopt her and call her Sarah."

"Babies aren't just cute and cuddly, Amanda. You can't *keep* them as if they were kittens. And they grow up."

"I know all that. But don't you like her, Dad? Don't you think she's adorable?" Amanda put her finger in the baby's hand and Sarah grasped it and opened her eyes. "Look, Dad, she wants to stay with us, see?"

Mr. Atkins smiled. "She certainly is lovely. But babies cost a lot of money."

Amanda frowned as she thought about that. She stroked the back of Sarah's hand. "But she's just here. She doesn't have any parents. We don't have to *buy* her."

"I didn't mean to buy. I meant babies are expensive to raise. There are clothes and food and doctor's bills, and glasses and braces and more clothes, summer camps and pony clubs and later on, university— I think that if you don't have enough money to give babies the right start in life, you're better off not having them."

Amanda could feel a lump of pain growing in her throat. She had to speak around it. "I thought you always said the best things in life were free. A baby's a best thing. Loving a baby is best. Does love cost?" She couldn't go on.

"Oh, sweetie." Mr. Atkins put his arm around

Amanda and tried to pull her near him, but she was stiff. "Love *is* the most important thing, but sometimes it's not enough."

"We have enough money—don't we?"

"For the three of us, not for four."

"She wouldn't cost much now, and I'd get a job. I could deliver papers and babysit and I'd even sell my bike—"

"It's useless to talk this way. We don't know a thing about this baby. Probably her parents will turn up."

"No they won't."

"You *are* very definite. Do you know something you're not telling us?"

"Well, I feel it in my bones. That's what you say when it's good fishing weather."

Mr. Atkins laughed and rubbed the top of the baby's head.

"You would like to adopt her, wouldn't you, Dad —if we can't find her parents?"

"I can think of worse things than another baby around the house. The first was very satisfactory." He smiled at Amanda and she felt warm inside. She allowed her head to rest on his shoulder. "You must want this baby very much"— Amanda nodded—"but it's not that easy. It's sort of like buying a horse. The initial cost is not so great as the cost of feeding and stabling and shoeing—"

"And a saddle and bridle." Amanda paused. "It doesn't seem fair. We're not that poor—Hey!" She sat up and looked at her father. "Maybe Mum'll sell her paintings for thousands next week and then we can afford Sarah—and we can buy Flame!"

Mr. Atkins pressed his lips together and sighed the sort of sigh Amanda knew meant he was getting tired of the conversation.

Mrs. Atkins came back into the room. "The police say they'll be along as soon as they can. They may not be able to reach any foster parents to look after the baby tonight, and wondered if we'd keep her until morning if they can't make other arrangements. So I said she could stay here tonight. Just tonight, mind!"

"Yippee! She can sleep in my room!"

"Amanda!" her mother said. "You mustn't yell like that around babies. See, she's crying."

"I'm sorry, Sarah." Amanda rubbed the baby's back.

"And do stop calling her Sarah. We can't keep her so don't get attached to her."

Amanda looked up in time to see a strange expression on her father's face. "You know," he said, "we haven't thought about another baby in a long time."

Mrs. Atkins frowned. "It's out of the question. We aren't set up for a baby and we can't afford it. I gave away all Amanda's things and I'm in my studio or out all day. And Amanda's too old to be a playmate."

"I don't want a playmate," Amanda said. "I want a sister—this sister. And I don't care how old she is or if she gets into my things or what happens. I'd look after her and I'll get a job and buy her a crib."

Mr. Atkins smiled. "It's not necessary for you to go to work, Amanda. Your mother and I will talk about it. Privately."

Mrs. Atkins looked from her husband to her daughter to the baby. "But," she said, "but—but—" Then she sat down.

"She is lovely, isn't she, Mum?"

"She is that." Mrs. Atkins gently took the baby from her husband.

Amanda fell asleep that night staring at Sarah sleeping beside her on an improvised bed made of pillows. Sarah didn't wake till six in the morning, and Amanda heated a bottle and took the baby into her own bed to feed her. She felt extremely happy. Sarah gurgled and cooed in a way that made Amanda think she was happy too.

Later Amanda took the baby into her parents' bedroom and all four snuggled in the bed.

"You know," Mr. Atkins said dreamily, "I'm tired of going to work day in and day out. If we had lots of money, I would only work a little bit." He laughed. "Then I could stay home and look after a baby too."

Amanda stared at her father for a very long time.

12

Soapflakes here I come

After breakfast Mr. and Mrs. Atkins took their coffee into the living room. Sarah went back to sleep on her improvised bed and Amanda dug out the tube of purple toothpaste. She twisted the orange cap, then had to squeeze very hard to make the bubble appear. The toothpaste was almost all gone. She rolled the tube up from the bottom so the very last bit could emerge.

"If I wished for money, would you graduate?" she asked when the genie appeared.

"Money! That's the most wishable thing!" The genie would have been shouting if his voice hadn't shrunk so much. "The Master loves it! Pieces of eight. Spanish doubloons. Or diamonds and pearls. How about sunken treasure?"

"It has to be spendable money like dollars."

"Well, if you insist. A money tree in the yard or a roomful of bills. I can make them float down from the ceiling! I'll get started right now!"

"You haven't learned a thing, have you?" Amanda interrupted. "My mum and dad would have a fit if the house filled up with dollar bills. The money has to come in an unsuspicious way."

"An oil well in your back yard?"

Amanda shook her head.

"A rich uncle could leave it to you in his will."

"I don't have any rich uncles."

"I could deposit it to your parents' bank account."

Amanda looked thoughtful for a minute, then shook her head. "They'd think someone had made a mistake."

"A kind stranger could give it to you."

"They'd just give it back."

"Jumping Geniacs! What do you want me to do?"

Amanda shrugged.

Both were silent for a few minutes. Then the genie said, "I told you it was no use. Soapflakes here I come." His lower lip jutted out in a quivery pout.

"Don't start crying—think. I don't even know how much money to wish for."

"You probably think a hundred dollars is enough. Just because you're a little kid!"

"You say that once more, genie, and I'll chuck you in the garbage! I won't even try to help you!"

"Help *me*? I'm giving *you* the money!"

"*You* need it to graduate!"

The genie looked away. "Well, don't trifle. If you

won't let me make pieces of eight or Spanish doubloons, at least wish for a million dollars. That's a
nice round figure."

"Okay."

"You're sure you don't want it to appear in the
living room? Thousands of hundred-dollar bills? It's
very spectacular."

"That would be fun." Amanda smiled. "But I just
know my parents don't like magic. They're having
enough trouble trying to decide about babies. They
will adopt Sarah, won't they?"

"Yes, yes, I told you I fixed that up yesterday.
My job would be so much easier if people liked
magic, but nobody likes anything spectacular nowadays." The genie thought for a minute. "Your parents could win the money."

"Hey, that's great! My dad's always buying lottery tickets! He could win a million dollars!"

"Go find out if he has a ticket and when the draw
is. And do it quickly. I'm evaporating . . . " The genie
could only whisper now. Amanda had to hold the
bubble to her ear.

"Can't you read his mind?"

"I'm too weak."

Amanda ran into the living room. Her parents
stopped talking and looked at her. Amanda opened
her mouth, then realized she couldn't ask her father
if he had a ticket for a lottery he was going to win.
It was too suspicious.

118

She dashed down to the hall to her parents' bedroom, where her father's wallet lay on top of his dresser. She fumbled through it and finally found the ticket. She dashed back to her room.

"The draw isn't until next month," she said.

"That's okay," the genie whispered. "You won't get the money until then, but I can put it in my report if I do the heavy work now. Things like that are covered in the month of wishing, not getting." He looked thoughtful. "And Amanda, I'll make sure Mr. Sutherland will sell you Flame, too. His business will improve and he'll have to move to Toronto and leave Flame behind." The genie smiled. "You're really not so bad—for a little kid."

"Thanks a lot—but won't I ever see you again?" Amanda asked. She felt very sad. "Won't I find out if you graduate?"

"Oh, I'll graduate now, I know that." The genie's voice trailed away as the purple bubble evaporated.

Amanda was left sitting on the floor holding an empty, squished and battered toothpaste tube. She carefully unrolled and straightened the tube, smoothing it with her hands. She began to cry. For all his practical jokes, she'd become used to having her own genie and a wish every day. Life had not been boring since she'd found the toothpaste in Mr. Fung's store. She just hoped the genie would graduate and be happy.

In spite of all his jokes, the genie had left her

Flame and a baby sister, and now her family would be rich. Her father could stay home and look after Sarah while her mother painted, and in a while Mr. Sutherland would sell her Flame.

Amanda moved over beside the sleeping baby and gently took her hand. Sarah's eyes opened. They were a very deep purple. Amanda hadn't noticed it before. The baby stared at Amanda and waved her hands about. She pointed one of them at the battered tube of toothpaste, and as Amanda watched in amazement, the tube lifted itself out of her hand. Sarah was certainly no ordinary baby, Amanda decided, but then she hadn't come in a very ordinary way, either.

Maybe Sarah could teach her how to make things move like that, Amanda thought. And she could teach Sarah lots too. How to walk and read, and when she was a lot bigger, how to ride Flame. She would look after her and keep her safe and let her help bake cookies.

The toothpaste tube was floating around the room, doing dips and dives and loop-the-loops as Sarah waved her hands. Amanda laughed and stuck out her hand to catch it, but each time it came close to her the tube veered away. Then she just about had it; one finger touched it but the tube looped up in the air and came down hard across Amanda's knuckles. Amanda cried and put her knuckles to her mouth. Sarah laughed and Amanda frowned. She would have to teach Sarah it wasn't nice to laugh when someone got hurt.

As she looked at the baby, Amanda continued to frown. Sarah's hair seemed to have acquired a distinctly green tinge overnight—or maybe it was just a reflection from the curtains . . .

Sarah had the toothpaste tube in her mouth and some of the writing was coming off on her lips. Amanda leaned over to pick the paint away before the baby swallowed it and suddenly, right then, and right in front of her eyes, Sarah disappeared.

At first Amanda didn't believe it. She sat in the same position and looked at the tumbled blankets. She looked around the room in case Sarah was floating like the toothpaste. But nowhere was there any sign of the baby. Amanda still couldn't believe it. She didn't *want* to believe it. She looked in her closet to see if the doll was back; it was not. Sarah had gone.

The genie had not kept his part of the bargain. Amanda's despair changed to total fury. She really had thought he would keep his last promise. She really had trusted him. And then her anger changed to fear: now she would have to tell her parents the whole story.

13
Case closed

"Sarah's gone!" Amanda blurted, and started to cry.

Mr. and Mrs. Atkins looked at her quietly and calmly, with little smiles on their faces, as if she had announced that tea was ready or that on sunny days the sky was blue.

"She's gone, don't you understand? He tricked me, he didn't keep his promise!"

"What do you mean 'gone'? And who is 'he'? The baby's too young to crawl. She can't be gone!" Mr. Atkins went into Amanda's room. He looked at the improvised bed on the floor, looked all around the room, felt the blankets, pulled up Amanda's bedspread and looked under it, just as she had done. He opened the closet and even moved the wastepaper basket. "Okay, Amanda, this isn't funny. Where have you put the baby?"

Amanda continued to cry. "I haven't put her anywhere, that's what I'm trying to tell you. She's just disappeared."

"Babies don't just disappear."

"Yes, they do."

Mr. Atkins hurried down the hall with Amanda after him. He looked in all the bedrooms, the den, the bathroom, the kitchen, the dining room, and ended up back in the living room. "She's right, the baby's gone," he said to Mrs. Atkins.

"But she can't have gone anywhere. Even if she's a very early crawler she must still be in the house." Mrs. Atkins jumped up and searched the house, and this time both Amanda and her father trailed along. Eventually they arrived back in the living room.

"She's been kidnapped!" Mrs. Atkins cried. "What do we do? When did you last see her, Amanda?"

Amanda sat down. "She hasn't been kidnapped— at least not in the way you mean. The genie must have taken her back."

She looked at both her parents. "You'd better sit down. I'm sure you won't believe me, but I'd better tell you. Just please don't get mad, and don't interrupt until I'm finished. I'm not going to lie. This all happened."

She took a deep breath. "I had a genie. He was in a toothpaste tube. When you sent me to the store, Mum, the last time I posed for you, that's when I got him. It was an accident, I didn't mean to buy a genie—though he said I must have meant to since genies don't get bought by just anybody."

Now that Amanda had started to tell her story she felt surprisingly calm. Even though it was important to her that her parents believe her, there was not much she could do to *make* them believe other than telling the story. But her parents saw her calmness and that did more than anything to convince them she was not making it all up.

"If you have a genie, where is it? Show it to us," her father broke in.

"I *had* a genie. He's gone. His time was up."

"What does this have to do with the baby?" Mr. Atkins asked.

Mrs. Atkins had been staring at Amanda with an even more peculiar expression than that of her husband. She turned to him. "Hush. Let her tell the story and don't keep interrupting."

"Just one thing, Amanda," her father said. "*Where* is the baby? We have to find her!"

"I don't know where she is. She's just gone, but somehow I know she's safe." Mr. Atkins did not look convinced, but he let Amanda continue.

"I guess she was at least part genie and not all baby, and I bet she's either turned back into a doll or has gone wherever genies go. See, he made her from a doll because he stole the horse—Flame—and he couldn't make her out of nothing. But he promised this time he'd make me a sister and he wouldn't play any jokes! And to think I helped him graduate! I bet we don't even get the money!" Her eyes filled with tears and she wiped them on the back of her hand. Mrs. Atkins got up and gave her a kleenex, then sat on the arm of her chair and put her arms around Amanda.

"Your father looks most confused. Why don't you start at the beginning?"

So Amanda told the whole story, simply and calmly. When she got to the part where the horse appeared in her room, both her parents laughed. And when she came to the end, both shared her indignation that the genie had not kept his part of the bargain.

"I know it's hard to believe," Amanda finished, "and I don't even have proof to show you. Sarah took the toothpaste tube and that's all I had. Do you believe me?"

"Well . . . I—" Mr. Atkins began.

"Wait a minute," Mrs. Atkins interrupted. "I'll be right back."

"It's very far-fetched," Mr. Atkins said. "I've never heard of anything like it. You're either an extremely good storyteller or else it is true. But it can't be! And I can't believe the baby disappeared." He looked around the room as if expecting to see Sarah cooing and gurgling in her basket.

"I can't believe it myself any more," Amanda said

sadly. "I don't have a thing left. Flame is really Mr. Sutherland's and now Sarah's gone, and we probably won't win the money—some genie."

Mrs. Atkins came down from her studio carrying a large canvas. "Is this what the genie looked like, Amanda?"

She held up an exact and realistic portrait of the genie staring out of a pale purple background. His eyes were half-closed as if he would like to be asleep, but worry had kept him awake. He held his pipe in one hand and the fingers of the other were poised to flick a spark into the bowl. His loincloth was exactly the right red and his hair the right shade of green. It was a very different picture from those Mrs. Atkins usually painted.

"That's him exactly! Where did you see him?"

Mrs. Atkins propped the canvas against the coffee table and sat down where she could look at it. "I didn't see him. That is, I didn't see him in the daytime. I didn't even know he was in the house. I dreamed him—at least, I thought I did, about three nights in a row. He appeared out of nowhere and kept looking at me as if he wanted to know something about me. He never spoke, never did anything, just kept looking at me--like that. So I painted him a couple of weeks ago."

Amanda smiled. "It's exactly the way he looked when I told him to stop playing jokes, and threatened to show him to you so you'd make him pose.

He thought you sounded horrible—I guess he wanted to see for himself. How come you didn't paint him the way you paint me? He looks real and I never do."

"I don't know. This was the way I had to paint him, exactly as he seemed. But then, of course, you are real and he's not—not in the same way, that is. Maybe I was trying to get the magic of you—"

"The *real* me," Amanda interrupted.

"—mnnm, and this is the *essence* of genie, looking real. But he's not real—not the way we are. I don't know. I don't know what's real and what's not. I don't know the difference between magic and artistic inspiration—I thought the genie was some inspiration of mine; I didn't think he existed. But I did know this was how I had to paint him."

"You have to believe me now, Dad," Amanda said, "now there's a picture of him."

Mr. Atkins looked totally confused. "I can't believe it—I mean, I *know* it can't be true. I mean, I *don't know* it can be true . . . It's just not the sort of thing I can know. I can't really believe it." He paused. "I guess the best I can do is not disbelieve."

"That's okay, isn't it, Amanda?" Mrs. Atkins said with a smile. "There are lots of things we don't know with our minds, things we have to take on faith—or put into a holding pattern in our minds until we have more knowledge."

"You mean I could have told you about the genie

right away in the beginning? I didn't have to get in trouble for the fish? I could just have taken Flame out the kitchen door and not had to hide him in the bathroom?" Both her parents smiled. "But I thought you'd say I was crazy! I didn't think you'd believe in magic!"

"I might not have believed," Mr. Atkins said, "but I sure would have liked to see him—especially coming out of the toothpaste tube!"

The Atkinses continued to stare at the portrait in silence for some time. Then Mrs. Atkins looked out the window and leaped to her feet. "Good grief, here comes a policeman! What are we going to say? They'll think we murdered the baby!"

Mr. Atkins jumped up too. "Oh, I'd completely forgotten! We'll tell them ... "

"What?" asked Mrs. Atkins, pacing back and forth.

"The truth?" Amanda offered, but her parents ignored her.

"Tell them whoever left the baby came back!" Mr. Atkins said.

'Tell them it was a mistake," Mrs. Atkins said.

"Tell them I was playing a joke," Amanda said.

All three Atkinses looked at each other. Amanda was about to suggest they hide in the basement when the doorbell rang. Mr. Atkins took a deep breath and opened the door.

"Yes, good day," the policeman said. "You reported an abandoned baby?"

"All a mistake, Officer, all a mistake. The person came back for her. Changed her mind, I guess. She was playing a joke." Mr. Atkins smiled and rocked up and down on his toes.

"She was only temporarily deluded," Mrs. Atkins added. "Upset. She—uh—had a fight with her husband."

Amanda stared at her parents. She had never heard them lie before.The genie seemed to have a way of making people do things they didn't usually do.

The policeman stepped into the house and took out his notebook. "This sounds most peculiar. What is the woman's name? I'll have to check it out."

Mr. and Mrs. Atkins looked at each other. "We—uh—didn't find out her name. It was all rather sudden."

Amanda could see the policeman did not believe her parents. She wouldn't have believed them either. She stepped forward. "I did it, sir. I wanted a baby so much I—borrowed one. It wasn't my parents' fault. She's gone back now."

The policeman looked at Amanda. Mr. and Mrs. Atkins looked at Amanda. The policeman frowned at all of them. "This all sounds very odd," he said. "First you phone to report an abandoned baby, then you don't phone to report it isn't abandoned. You didn't know what your daughter was doing. Are you sure you haven't all been having fun at the expense of the Police Department? That is a very serious offense."

"Not at all, Officer. And we have dealt with our daughter. It's unfortunate we made the report in the first place, but we were rather confused."

"How do I know that? How do I know *you* haven't abandoned the baby somewhere else? Where it might not be found for a long time?"

"Oh, that wouldn't happen," Amanda said.

"You'd better give me the details just in case. This might warrant an investigation. It sounds serious." The policeman crossed to the couch, flipped open his notebook, produced a pen and sat down. He caught sight of the portrait of the genie still propped against the table. He looked at it briefly, raised his eyebrows, frowned and dropped his gaze to the notebook. But immediately he looked up at the portrait again, and then continued to stare at it. As he did, his expression changed from one of distaste and disbelief to surprise, and then to one of satisfaction. Amanda and her parents watched his face and exchanged anxious looks with one another.

The policeman stood up. "Yes, well, everything seems to be in order. You had a baby abandoned on your doorstep, but the baby was claimed. It is well looked after and your daughter did nothing wrong. I would say that is that. Case closed. And I quite understand how it is you didn't happen to report back in. Sorry to have bothered you. Goodbye."

The Atkinses continued to stare at one another after the police car had driven away. Finally Mr. Atkins closed the front door. "Do you think he flipped his wig? Went bonkers?"

Mrs. Atkins collapsed in a chair, her feet stuck out in front of her. "I don't know. I don't care. He left. We're not arrested."

"But I wonder what made him change his mind."

"I did," said the genie's voice.

"Where are you?" asked Amanda.

"Where's who?" asked Mrs. Atkins.

"The genie. He just said, 'I did.' Didn't you hear him?"

"No," said Mrs. Atkins.

"Neither did I," agreed her husband.

"Can't they hear you?" asked Amanda.

"Only you can, and you know where I am."

Amanda looked at the painting. The genie was bobbing gently within the confines of his portrait. But now he was wearing a small red hat.

"Can't they see you?"

"No, you're the only one who can see and hear me and I had to get special dispensation to come back."

131

"I'm so glad you did," Amanda said sarcastically. "You've been a big help. I sure hope you didn't graduate—you couldn't even keep your last promise, could you? You had to take Sarah away. And I just about got into the biggest trouble ever!"

"That's why I've come back. I'm *so* sorry about Sarah. I didn't know I couldn't make a human baby. I can only make a baby genie. I didn't know. I'm sorry."

"I bet you are! I bet you knew all along she wouldn't be real. You just couldn't resist tricking me again! And after I helped you too!"

"Say what you like, Amanda. It's no more than I deserve and you did help me. I did graduate. See my graduation hat?" He took it off and admired it, then put it back on. "They left some things out of the manual and making babies was one of them. Technically, it should have worked. I had an object to start with, one that was the right form even, but I checked with the Master. Genies can only give life to make genies, just as humans can only make humans. Cows can't have piglets and bears can't have foals—genies can't make human babies. I didn't know. I really wanted to do it for you, but I guess your only hope for a sister is for your parents to want one. Anyway, you wouldn't have liked having a baby genie about—there's nothing trickier or more full of pranks than a baby genie. We mellow as we get older."

132

"Oh, sure," Amanda said. She was still angry with him, but he looked so sorrowful she had to believe him. "I still think it was *mean* giving us Sarah and then having that happen," she said, but her voice had lost some of its conviction. "Now all I have is neat handwriting."

"And memories. We did have fun, didn't we, in spite of my little games?"

Amanda nodded.

"And Sarah reminded your parents how nice babies are." Amanda nodded again. "And you will have Flame all to yourself in a month." Another nod. "And because your mother's an artist you have a picture of me. *That*, you know, is highly irregular. I just hope the Master Genie never finds out."

Amanda smiled. For a second there was a touch of the old genie in his voice. Everything he did, it seemed, was highly irregular. If she'd been the Master she didn't think she'd have graduated him. "But you're a Master Genie yourself now," she said.

His cheeks formed bright purple bumps above a wide smile. "Why yes, I am, aren't I? I keep forgetting. No toothpaste, no soap powder, I can just float. And I'd better float off now. Genies are not to return to the scene of a previous sojourn, page 58 in the manual. Thanks again, Amanda, and I'm sorry about Sarah. She sends her regards, by the way. Who knows, maybe when she's an apprentice you'll meet up with her—and I'm going to put something

133

in the manual about babies right away. Goodbye."

The canvas again showed his portrait the way Mrs. Atkins had painted it. "Oh, for goodness sake," Amanda said. "I forgot to ask if we'll still win the lottery!"

"I guess we'll have to wait to find out," Mr. Atkins said.

And Amanda thought that after all the excitement of the past month there was something relaxing about "waiting to find out" just like everyone else.

Sandy Frances Duncan

Sandy Frances Duncan has written a variety of books for both children and adults, some as Frances Duncan. *Cariboo Runaway*, her first novel, is the story of two children who trek to the Cariboo gold fields in search of their father. *Kap-sung Ferris* is about a young skater whose promising career is shaken when she begins to feel she doesn't fit in because she's adopted. Duncan's two adult novels were followed by *Listen to Me, Grace Kelly*, in which twelve-year-old Jess tries to sort out her confusion about her father's death with the help of her imaginary confidante, a glamourous movie star.

Born in Vancouver, Duncan now lives on an island with two cats, numerous raccoon visitors and a resident deer who eats the roses. Among other books, she is working on a sequel to *The Toothpaste Genie*.